INTEGRITY, 130,000 BC

THE CERUTTI MASTODON SITE

BONNYE MATTHEWS

Award Winning Writer
of Prehistoric Fiction

PUBLICATION
CONSULTANTS
We Believe In The Power Of Authors

PO Box 221974 Anchorage, Alaska 99522-1974
books@publicationconsultants.com—www.publicationconsultants.com

ISBN: 978-1-59433-845-8
eISBN: 978-1-59433-846-5

Library of Congress Catalog Card Number: 2018967610

Manufactured in the United States of America.

Other Books by Bonnye Matthews

Winds of Change Novel Series
Ki'ti's Story, 75,000 BC
Manak-na's Story, 75,000 BC
Zamimolo's Story, 50,000 BC
Tuksook's Story, 35,000 BC
The SealEaters, 20,000 BC

Archaeological Sites Series

Freedom, 250,000 BC
Courage, 48,000 BC

Non-Fiction

People in the Americas before the Last Ice Age Glaciation Concluded: An Emerging Western Hemisphere Population Origin Paradigm

Contents

Acknowledgements

Without the assistance of several people, *Integrity, 130,000 BC* would not exist. These people are my brother, Randy Matthews, Sally Sutherland, Pat Meiwes, and Rebecca Goodrich. Each contributed far in excess of what could be expected or hoped for based on family, friendship, or love of reading. Thank you to the Mat-Su College Librarians who provided such gracious interlibrary loan service for materials that helped tremendously with background for this book. Finally, thanks to Keith Chan, PhD for providing the image of the standing tusk.

8

Exordium

Muz invited me to meet. I accepted. I always accept. From the window I saw the flames in the firepit blazing. I grabbed a quilt from the arm of the sofa. The yard was littered with yellow, brown, and orange leaves, tossed by the breeze that gusted intermittently, despite the brief rainfall earlier in the day.

I hurried, eager to see Muz once again. It had been quite a while. His arms, thrown open wide, welcomed me and my returned hug, my quilt momentarily lost on the ground. Muz has a warmth that has nothing to do with temperature. His arms enclosed me with his huge vitality, wrapping us momentarily, as if in an energizing bubble. I'm so short; he is so tall. When we sit together, the difference is not as noticeable.

At the firepit I sat on my rock, legs crossed, entirely wrapped in my warm quilt, held together with my chilled hands. Muz wore only his boar skin, a kilt-like skirt, a grayish look to it now, because of its need for a wash and the age and wear of the garment. It just covered his knees in its length. His bony chest was bare to the elements, hairless. He never seemed to feel the cold, instead, he exuded warmth. Sometimes, I wondered whether, if needed, he could start a fire with his own warmth. Maybe that's how he set up the firepit. The deboned tail on the side of his skirt looked the same, showing no additional signs of wear since last I saw him.

The wrinkled old man descended more gracefully than I to a seated position, folded his crossed legs, and put his hands to the fire, as if to warm them. Hands to the fire was not a gesture of his being cold; it was a moment between him and fire, as if they were friends. His dark eyes reflected the light of the fire, dancing with glints to match the color of the leaves. A gust of wind blew his long glossy white hair, his sparkling eyes momentarily hidden. The fire spat, and tiny specks from a shift in the wood rose upward to the stars above, where white shape-shifting aurora ribbons glided soundlessly, transparently covering the stars overhead.

This time a scent of evergreens accompanied Muz. Only a few evergreens grew in my birch-, aspen-, alder-, and cottonwood-filled yard. He withdrew his hands from the fire and riveted me with his obsidian eyes. Smile wrinkles deepened about his eyes and mouth. It's as if in one look he knew what passed in my life since we last met. It struck me as spooky the first time he did that, but no longer is that so. Now I welcome it, knowing it saved much time, and he cared about me and wanted to know. I didn't ask what has happened in his life. He would tell me, if it pleased him for me to know. Muz smiled. His mouthful of teeth looked really old but are fully functioning.

He stretched out his hands and held within the space between them an image of the earth. I saw the place where he pointed. It's what today is Southern California. Perhaps near San Diego.

Muz said, "Estimate the time 130,000 years ago."

I didn't question. I simply watched the earth image morph to a landscape view between his hands. The scene unfolded. Trees swayed at the edge of the forest and a young male mastodon emerged unsteadily to an open area. He had a broken tusk. Part of the tip dangled, still firmly attached. What must have been a wetland appeared off to the side of the forest. Green vegetation was interspersed among the brown crusts of the now parched soil where cattails, rushes, palmetto type plants, and ferns were drying up. Evidently, shallow water recently filled the area. It appeared as though something had sucked the area dry.

Mysteriously, I was certain of things I had no way to know. The mastodon, in late adolescence, had been on his own about half a year. He walked unsteadily with great effort to a grassy area, as if terribly intoxicated. Something was desperately wrong. My concern grew, though I watched an image out of time, not a currently living mastodon—or did I?

The great beast stumbled and eased itself to the ground, as if in slow motion. He appeared devoid of all will to live. Birds squawked, fluttering in the trees. I watched the mastodon die. I saw its eye lose focus and stare blindly upwards. I felt overcome by profound sadness when the great beast heaved up its last exhalation. The speed of its death startled me. A solitary vulture hovered above at a great elevation. The bird must have been tracking the great mastodon, aware of its fate.

This was an extraordinary way for Muz to begin his storytelling. I looked at his face, questioning, wordlessly.

He said, "Mastodon lost integrity."

"What?" I blurted out without thinking, my quilt falling from my grasp and exposing my neck to the chilly breeze. I was unprepared. Somehow the word integrity didn't fit. The mastodon had lost his life. Integrity? Do animals have integrity?

"Integrity, wholeness. Wholeness. Without, broken." He shrugged his shoulders.

I didn't understand at all. His way of speaking and his choice of words threw me off balance.

Muz rested his hands on his thighs. He looked at me, and then his eyes focused overhead. I wondered whether he gazed upon the aurora or something else, maybe something I didn't see. He cleared his throat, still looking above.

"Mastodon alone." He paused. "Alone—way of life for mastodon male." Muz paused. "He thirsted." Muz paused. "All mastodons thirsted in dry time." He paused. "Mastodon drank bad water. Thirst overwhelmed. Not know better. Kept drinking bad water." He paused, his words were choppy. "Bad water broke mastodon." Muz paused. "Mastodon lost integrity—die." After some time, Muz said, "Without integrity all die—living things and things that do not live. Integrity holds all together. Rock break apart as time pass. Turn to dirt." Muz scooped up some dirt. He let it begin to slip through his dry, wrinkled fingers. "You lose integrity; you die; you turn to dirt. Same mastodon, same you." The dirt had gone from his hand back to the ground.

I wondered at that. I was still hung up on non-living things dying. How could non-living things die? I didn't ask. He expected my brain to find the meaning of his words. Why was he using choppy words as sentences? I stopped trying to understand. In time it would become clear. "Same mastodon, same you." One thing was clear. Short choppy words stuck.

Muz continued gazing above. I looked up to try again to see what he saw. I could not find anything remarkable. Between his hands I saw the mastodon carcass. Above, I could detect nothing but the aurora making its braiding pathways directly overhead, making curtains off to the north, making itself seen, but not clouding out the stars. They were clearly visible. How wonderful if people could do the same. I looked down and saw vultures on the carcass of the mastodon. I thought of integrity applied to the aurora, the stars beyond, the solar system in which we live, the earth on which I sat, the mastodon carcass, the rock beneath me, myself. Integrity held all together. It was a new thought for me. Then, my question: integrity? I thought I had known the meaning of the word. Holding things together? The idea of glue failed to work. Glue mends broken things. Broken things lost integrity when they broke. So, integrity is before broken, something whole or complete, the way it should be. That fit with my prior definition, as if that mattered. Before breaking there was integrity, not after. If one lost integrity, according to Muz, death followed. Could some people lose integrity and continue on living as the mastodon for a short time, being walking dead? Still functioning, but dead, like the staggering mastodon? Could we recognize alive from dead?

Muz began the story still focused above. No longer were his words choppy. My neck tired from my trying to find what might interest him above. I watched his face. I moved through the story with him as he told it, images no longer showing between his hands. I felt the story environment, smelled it, saw it, touched it, tasted it, sensed it—I was there. In storytelling he left nothing to chance interpretation. Muz was back to normal, speaking in complex sentences with great deliberation and crystal clarity.

When the firepit encircled white-edged, crumbled cinders, Muz smiled, rose, touched my shoulder, leaving a trace of his special warmth even through the quilt. He walked off in an aura of golden light, entrusting me with this tiny part of the story to tell—the part about the people—a story from the past shared in the present for me to share for the future. The story failed to change over time. It is as true today as 130,000 years ago. People are people are people are people.

I lingered at the firepit. This task was greater than some others. I watched the aurora this time white and green, a hint of purple. The activity of it had increased. A tiny spot moved far up in the sky. A satellite? There are so many now. The spell Muz created took a long time to dissipate. Finally, I rose and carried the quilt back inside. The sun began to rise behind me. It was quite a night.

Dedication

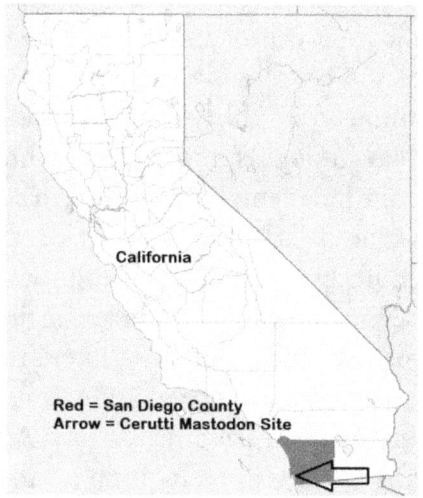

Cerutti Mastodon Site

I dedicate this book to the Cerutti Mastodon Site at San Diego, California, where about 130,000 BC humans broke bones to harvest marrow, bone, maybe some ivory, and tooth enamel from a fresh mastodon carcass. The bones were broken using a round cobble as a hammerstone to hit bone placed over a flat rock, the anvil. The humans did not live at the site, but rather they came to it for harvesting materials to carry back to their home. Bones and ivory could have been used for tools, weapons, possibly adornment or other significant items, and to add to fires to extend burning time. The mastodon teeth that were broken were likely for mining tooth enamel, useful as tools for cutting or scraping. The dental pulp of teeth has some nutritional value, so that may also have been what the humans were seeking. This was a sealed site, meaning it had not been disturbed until roadway construction work exposed it in 1992.

The site sits on a sandy silt bed in a low-energy river environment in thirty-nine feet of Pleistocene sediment. Paleontologists recovered over three hundred bones and bone fragments from a young male mastodon at the site. One tusk lay horizontally on the ground, and another, likely by human intention, was arranged vertically. Several ribs and vertebrae, fragile bones, at the site remained unbroken. It is interesting to note that there was no appearance of animals having killed the mastodon or eaten from the carcass. A bear could not have broken a leg bone by biting through it, but gnaw marks would show animal presence. There were no scavenger marks from any carnivore on the bones.

There were round pegmatite cobbles and flat andesite rocks from the east at the site. Andesite and pegmatite rocks were not an original part of the mastodon site geology. These rocks were carried to the site, not transported by rivers, since the area of the site was a slow-moving river environment, incapable of transporting such rocks.

Cerutti Mastodon Tusk Tip—White Line Shows Ground
Level Above Which Part of the Tusk Stood Upright
(Image courtesy of Keith Chan, PhD)

Most of the broken bones were three inches thick, not something a mastodon could easily break by treading on it or by a bear's biting into it. Paleontologists found two concentrations of spiral-fractured bones and broken molar fragments, characteristic of human harvesting, surrounding flat rocks used as anvils. Where bones had been broken, the fragments could be fitted back together, a finding that would have been unlikely had the stream been a fast-moving current, where rocks could be slammed together and fragments swept away in the water.

The bone breakage is characteristic of green bone fracture by hammerstone, not by trampling by other mastodons or any other known means. Contemporaneous experimental hammerstone percussion on elephant and cow bones produce the exact pattern of breakage as found at the site. The fragile ribs and vertebrae at the site plus encrustation on the bones over time, which maintained their integrity with no signs of breakage, lead to the conclusion that neither the heavy equipment in road building nor mammoth trampling of the site can be used as viable arguments for non-human breaking of the bones.

Interestingly, there was other animal evidence near the site: horse, wolf, deer, and mammoth. None of those bones had been broken in the same manner.

There is no scientific debate over the date of the mastodon bones at 130,700 plus or minus 9.4 thousand years. Science in the USA regarding peopling of the Americas exists in a vacuum of decades of teaching that people were not in the Americas prior to the Holocene (12,000 to 11,500 years ago to present). The current debate involves belief over how the bones were broken. This part of the debate involves a lot of speculation that masquerades as skepticism. For example, in an online article in https://arstechnica.com/science/2018/02/debate-heats-up-over-whether-130000-year-old-bones-were-broken-by-humans/ you can read:

"But Baylor University anthropologist Joseph Ferraro and his colleagues argue that natural processes could also have been to blame. They say they've seen the same kinds of spiral fractures, impact notches, and flake scars on bones at other sites—like a group of 24,000-year-old mammoth bones at Inglewood Mammoth Site in Maryland, a group of 66,800-to-51,300-year-old mammoth bones at Waco Mammoth National Monument in Texas, and others dating all the way back to the Triassic Period."

"No one has ever even suggested human occupation at these sites. Instead, the fractures turned out to be the result of postmortem trampling by other mammoths, the weight of several meters of sediment, or heavy earth-moving equipment. And at many of those sites, paleontologists found stone cobbles similar to those at Cerutti."

When scientists have been taught that it's not possible for humans to be in the Americas before the Holocene, it sets them up not even to consider the possibility. Logic alone should warn that people cannot prove a negative. In the belief that was taught, logic failed. Consequently, those sites in Maryland,

Texas, and others should be revisited to rule out human intervention by science, not expectation— if it's not too late. The Triassic is irrelevant to the quoted argument above. There were no mastodons in the Triassic. Comparing dinosaur and mastodon behavior is comparing apples to oranges.

To assume postmortem elephant-type trampling, when that is contrary to their behavior, or that road equipment is to blame for the breakage strikes me as not skeptical but rather stretching an argument beyond reason. When a scientist or anyone goes into very old sites, they go with expectations from decades of teaching a belief that no people were in the Americas before 11,700 years ago, a belief that has stifled pursuit of science.

In the case of the Cerutti Mastodon age, that paradigm of recent peopling of the Americas falls apart when considering the encrustation that formed over these fossils. Had earth-moving equipment done the damage, they would have broken the encrustation that formed. That was not the case. There was no lack of integrity in the encrustation. How could one break massive bones without damaging the more fragile crust around them? The skepticism on this issue strikes me as disingenuous, naïve, or ignorant. It would improve science if skepticism required either (1) scientific rationale, based on real research, not opinion, or (2) silence.

Einstein's words are relevant: "If the facts don't fit the theory, change the theory."

Finally, 130,000 years was not only a different time but also it was in some respects a different place from what it is today. For those who are interested in the species described in this story, go to the SPECIES NOTES beginning on page 151.

Clan Genealogy

Note: Italic names are females, numerals are age at beginning of story.

		Sig 13			*Got 9*
		Elka 10			Mult 7
	Abu 31	Elog 10		Lum 27	*Bega 4*
	+	Dit 5		+	*Sera 2*
	Dal 28			*Bit 23*	Ahn 0
		Barg 11			
Geol 48	Hol 27	*Hawk 9*	**Tip 42**	*Reorg 24*	Ranu 9
+	+	*Fema*	+	+	Lop 7
Matta 50	*Koa 25*	Mot 4	***Fai 38***	Jin 27	Nett 3
		Dippi 0			Pica 0
		Swan 10		Elom 21	*Wit 4*
		Egrid 8		+	Tat 2
	Pogu 24	*Rim 6*		*Wat 18*	(in
	+	*Dule 4*			womb)
	Sum 28	*Flam 2*			

Acconomaku—Stranger from the East, a traveler
Teera—Stranger's Wolf
Mawanaba of Mul—Chief of Mul

PART ONE

Elog was deeply disturbed. He twisted the edge of his old leather skirt. Where it had torn and left a long finger-like piece of leather dangling, it was tantalizing and, he thought through fingertip motion not words, a great place to drain worry, as if worry could be removed somehow through the fingertips. Sweat rivered down his back where the sun shone on his tanned skin, protected only by a single dark brown braid. He and his ten-year-old twin, Elka, had disagreed over what they would do to contribute to clan integrity that day. He wanted to spear a deer, and she wanted to satisfy her curiosity regarding the area where they'd seen the huge dead-eater birds circling far in the distance two moons ago. With a wingspan more than twice the height of a man, these birds could be seen at quite a distance. Elka assured him they could reach the place of the dead animal by running there and back in less than a day.

Their grandfather, Geol, had said no one should go to that place to gather tool-making material, until he was ready. They had no need of more meat to smoke. They had already stashed a great quantity for times when meat would be scarce. There was a drought, but their nearby lake was holding its water level. At present meat was plentiful, for their lake drew animals, especially when other, smaller water sources dried up.

Geol wanted to wait until the meat, identified by the circling dead-eaters, had rotted or been adequately scavenged, so the bones would be more easily available to harvest. He had no interest in competing with scavengers for tool-making material. Worst of all, a hunter's find nearby of three dead-eater birds, dead for no apparent reason, bothered him—an omen of bad luck tied to the carcass, Geol thought. Jin, his cousin, had found the dead-eater birds lying on a hill near each other, and he left them untouched. You could eat animals that primarily ate plants, birds, eggs, but not animals that ate animals, not unless it was starving time. You never ate dead-eaters, dead in numbers for no apparent reason.

They hadn't seen the dead-eater birds for a long time. Not until a little while ago when the sky seemed filled with them all heading to one place. The dead animal must have been a large one, they all agreed.

Geol said they could go when he was ready. No one would cross him. Crossing Geol could affect clan integrity. Geol was the clan leader. Everyone owed him obedience. It was part of clan integrity. Elka wanted to go there against Geol's prohibition, and Elog did not know how to reason with her, other than to say it would be wrong. Likely punishable. His argument had been ineffective. Elog ripped the long leather finger from the bottom of his skirt. He hung it on a thin tree branch, thinking a bird might use it for nesting material.

It was high sun and Elka had been gone since early morning. In frustration Elog threw a pebble hard at a flat rock. It bounced back, hitting him in the knee. His knee bled, but the wound was not a bad loss of skin integrity. Elog was unsure what to do about Elka. He scanned the area for Sig, without success in locating his older brother.

Dal, his mother, called to him. "Where's Elka? She should be helping prepare our evening meal."

"I don't know," Elog admitted.

"What do you mean? You're always together." His mother, Dal, was shocked.

"We argued early this morning, and I haven't seen her since then."

His uncle, Hol, having overheard the words, added, "I always said they should have put her aside the day she was born."

"Hol, don't start that again!" Dal bitterly insisted. It was settled long ago. Dal realized too late that Elog had heard the words, carelessly tossed out by her brother-in-law.

"Only because she was born first," Hol sneered. "She affects our integrity. Always has."

Elog had no idea what they were talking about. He felt unsteady, as if the earth shook in confusion.

Hol continued, "She was only saved because it's the second twin who gets put aside, and he was a male. She was cursedly lucky." Hol had been picking his nose, finally dislodged the booger, and ate it.

Elog suddenly had a monstrous revelation, and it hurt him deeply. The realization that Elka would not be alive, had he been born first, was a clan rule beyond his comprehension. Who made such rules? he wondered. There had been times he'd wished to have been the first-born. This made him reevaluate his previous thoughts in the speed of a lightning strike. Surely, Elka made him thunder-roll angry from time to time, but she was part of him. If Elka died, he'd lose *his* integrity, of that he was certain. Did his uncle not understand? Elog held his thoughts to himself. He felt shattered.

Dal went to Abu, her husband, to let him know that Elka was missing. He and Hol, his brother, did not get along well, so he turned to his youngest brother, Sum, and distant cousin, Jin, for help. After they searched the perimeter, they found no trace of tracks leading away from their home. As soon as Geol, Abu's father, heard, he called the entire people together to learn whether anyone had seen Elka, and when was the last sighting. No one had seen her after early morning. Hawk, Hol's nine-year-old daughter, pointed in the direction that Abu realized would lead to the carcass, far in the distance. It could be near the small, slow stream that meandered through the sandy area off in the distance. Hunters knew it took almost a full day to reach it when trekking, if that were her destination.

Geol looked at Elog who had tried to make himself disappear. "Elog," he said, "Did Elka say anything to you about leaving?"

Elog sat up straight. He must tell all he knew, to do otherwise would cause him to lose his personal integrity and in this case might affect clan integrity.

"We argued over how to contribute to clan integrity today. I wanted to hunt deer. She wanted to visit the dead beast that the birds showed us. I never thought she might try to go there alone after I refused." Elog feared he might weep. He did not want to weep in front of the clan. He loved his sister and did not want any bad thing to happen to her. Elka could be difficult, but they had a bond, a strong one.

Geol was surprised that Elka might go to the place he'd wanted left alone. His granddaughter was always a surprise. He adored her because of it. This, however, might have gone too far. He would see. Had she no fear?

Abu looked at his cousin, Elom. "Will you drum the gathering signal?" he asked.

Elom nodded and went to the tree trunk they had cleared of bark in one place and carved out. The tree trunk sat on two rocks, giving it the resonance to transmit sound over large distances. He picked up the two large drumsticks and began the drum call to gather at home. One-two-three-four beats, then one-two-three, slower. Elom's well-developed arm muscles bulged as he applied all the force he could to create the sound. His back muscles stood out in ridges. He kept repeating the pattern for the count of ten. Then, he paused and repeated. The sound would travel far. He was concerned that, if the girl had indeed headed to the stream at a run, she might by now be out of hearing distance. It could take a day at a man's walk to reach the stream where they expected to find the dead animal. Elka, however, was athletic and ran often. Elom expected her run to have exceeded the normal hearing distance of the drum. It was humid, though, so there was a chance the sound would travel a bit further. Elom estimated it was unlikely, humidity or not, that she'd hear it.

The drum call brought several people in from their activities, but Elka did not return. Abu, her father, was becoming increasingly agitated.

"Dal, I need provisions for three to four days. Sum," he called out to his brother, "will you join me?"

Dal said, "Provisions for two, then, or three?" She saw Sum's nod. Abu held up three fingers, expecting to find Elka.

"Father?" Elog spoke quietly.

"No, you must stay here. Go with some of the men to hunt meat for the clan while I am gone. We will be two men fewer than normal. Stretch yourself to grow older in my absence." Abu spoke slowly while holding Elog's left shoulder with his large hand. He kept looking into his son's eyes as he spoke. Elog held his father's gaze, his disappointment sliding away at the thought of going on a real hunt with men. Abu would speak with Jin and Lum, his cousins, to get them to invite Elog to hunt with them that afternoon. He patted Elog's shoulder and turned to find his cousins to ask them to include his son on a hunt. There remained plenty of daylight. Even if unsuccessful, a quick hunt would do wonders for Elog.

Elog's sadness had been replaced with some happiness at the thought of hunting. Only Sig, his older brother, had ever hunted with the men. Elog suddenly realized that at ten, he was one of the older of the young people in the clan. Sig was the oldest at thirteen. Barg at eleven was second. Then Swan, Elka, and he were next at age ten. It struck him odd that he had never thought of his place in the clan as approaching manhood. He was filled with gratitude at his father's words, "Stretch yourself to grow older." He felt assurance surge through him. He could do that. He could stretch himself. Lots of special privileges came with manhood, but there was also a lot of responsibility. He began to see things a little differently.

Meanwhile, Elka was jogging. She had never in her life felt so free. She had a good sense of direction to the small river where she expected the dead beast to lie. Her expectation was a mastodon or mammoth, since they could reasonably attract so many of the enormous dead-eaters.

Her thoughts, however, mainly were focused on the jog. Elka kept watch around her, aware that predators could be anywhere, and she held tight to her spear. The rhythmic breathing was a pleasure to her, as were her strides. Her moves were as fluid as her thoughts, focused on the terrain and the destination with a joy that comes from covering great distance quickly. The land was not flat, and it contained many small ups and downs. The soil broke apart into dust beneath Elka's feet. As Elka continued on, she hummed a tune of few notes, playing with the patterns, enjoying the humming sound in relation to breathing and the sound of her heart.

A far distant sound like a drum momentarily pierced her mind, but she dismissed it as a memory or a waking dream to accompany her humming, not as something in the present. The sound was not repeated. She did not even slow down. Sometime later, Elka began to tire. The small river was ahead and she hurried to the edge. She would cool off, drink some water, and hunt crayfish, hoping quickly and easily to satisfy any hunger she might feel when she cooled.

As she walked around cooling down, Elka noticed a tree a little distance from where she arrived at the water. She went to the tree and found a small, straight stick a bit longer than her outstretched hand. Elka removed the bag she had tied to her waist. She chose the piece of sharp-edged mastodon tooth enamel to help remove the bark from the stick. She carved the tip to a point with it. The bag tied back to her waist, Elka walked to the water, while she poked the stick through two parallel holes in her tunic, like a third hand, these were cut into clothing as a holder of things. The stick was secured. She had cooled down. Elka sank to her knees, with two hands scooped up water, and drank it slowly until she thirsted no longer. She was surprised that it tasted better than their lake water. It was wonderful to feel the liquid brighten her sense of wellbeing. She had thirsted mightily. Elka looked around her. It was a day of wonderful blue sky and the travel had been joy filled, especially for one who loved to run. She was bursting with life and health. She had never been so distant from home, and she became aware that there was great beauty in other places.

Throwing her arms wide and circling while looking up, Elka cried out, "I would like to live right here. It fills me with wonder and joy! It's far from the forest edge, and I am overwhelmed by how big it is! What huge land, and the water is so good!" Her dark brown hair had loosened from the leather tie that held her single braid down her back. The wavy clean hair from the braid hung wild and free about her. Elka pulled hands full of her hair out to the side, looking down at her shadow, as if making a strange creature of herself. She made some screeching noises to create a voice for the shadow creature, and she flapped her arms, bending at the waist. She giggled at the shadow sight. She couldn't resist variations of shadow creation for a while.

She reached up and took hold of her hair with both hands. She pulled it behind her, but as soon as she let go, it was flying about again in the breeze. She had no memory of losing the leather strip that confined her braid end to a secure hold.

Elka sank to her knees and reopened the pouch at her waist. She wore a tunic to just below her knees. It was soft deerskin. Elka pulled out the same cutting tool she used to debark and shape the point of the stick and carefully cut off a straight piece of leather from the bottom of her tunic. She thought to herself how proud her mother would be at the straightness of the cut she'd made with her tiny tool. With some care, since she carried no comb, she rebraided her hair and confined the ends by wrapping and then tying the braid's end with the strip of leather. She tied it as tightly as possible. After putting away the pouch, Elka picked up her spear, reaching up to be sure she still had the small, pointed stick secured, and headed to the river's edge. When she arrived, she took her braid's end, soaked it, then tied the knot even tighter, knowing it would shrink even more when it dried. She didn't want to lose it again.

The river ran smoothly, though slowly, with pockets where the water collected in rounded pond-like groupings off to the side, and Elka began to look for crayfish in the slower, pooling water. There was some vegetation at the edge a little further up the river to the north. Elka was accustomed to catching crayfish from under rocks, but this river was silty, not rocky like the edge of their lake. She hoped there would be crayfish under the overhanging vegetation. She stepped as stealthily as possible, moving into the water from downriver so as not to loosen the silt more than necessary, for it would cloud the water quickly. Arriving first at the sedges, she parted the vegetation out of the way. The sedges growing tall and straight, were a disappointment, hiding no crayfish at all. She realized there was no room for sedges and crayfish together. Further up the river, yellow lotus, was more flexible and grew in the water—exactly what she hoped for. After almost giving up, Elka gently moved a few more of the large flat leaves and spotted a large crayfish. Heartened at finding potential food, she maintained patience and slowly moved toward it from the back. Finally, hardly breathing, she caught it by the tail and carapace, pinching it tight between her fingers and thumb, delighted. Caught that way, she could avoid the crayfish's pincers, and this one was showing its pincers wide open to the air. She liked its fierceness, while she smiled at its futile effort. It would have fought, had it any chance at a target. So as not to lose the crayfish, Elka went onshore a small distance where she stopped to spear it through the carapace. She stuck the end of the stick with the crayfish through the two slitted cuts in her tunic to carry it, until she was ready to eat it.

Elka returned to the river. She laid her weapon carefully on the bank, eager to find more food, for she was growing hungry. The spear was within easy reach. She extended her arm behind herself downstream and grabbed a yellow lotus flower. She knew these flowers were edible, so she ate two of the sets of petals and then another, along with tiny snails and anything else that might be lurking among the petals. A small tree frog in the third flower was not something she wanted to eat, so she tossed it back to the lotus leaves behind her. Elka was still hungry, but the flowers helped. Elka continued her search. Eventually, she found two more crayfish, each larger than the first. Again, Elka walked on shore with them before taking the stick from her tunic to spear them. She picked up her spear and went to the tree. On the way, Elka pulled a large handful of chickweed. She ate it on the way. She sat leaning against the tree and pulled the first crayfish from the stick. She twisted the carapace and tail until she felt the pop of separation. Elka tossed the carapace toward the water and took a moment to watch it float away. She split the tail and sucked the meat from it. In rapid succession she finished off the additional two tails. She preferred cooked crayfish, but she could eat them raw when necessary.

For the first time since she left home, Elka suddenly felt very much alone. She had experienced great freedom, but the tradeoff was the absence of her family, her clan. In an instant, she felt on the edge of panic. She experienced for the first time in her life what it was to be alone. She'd never felt such a horror. Night would come and where would she sleep? How would she stay warm? She'd considered none of those things. She didn't dare try to go home with dark coming on. She knew she could lose her way. What if a predator arrived? Elka's gut clenched up on her newly acquired food. She fought to calm herself. She had eaten and needed to keep her food inside.

Back at home, Elog had sought out his grand-mother, Matta. Matta could see things that others could not see, understood what confounded others, give guidance others found remarkable.

"What brings you here, Grandson?" Matta asked, sitting on a soft, fur-covered skin toward the middle of the shelter she shared with her husband, Geol. "Sit," she invited Elog. Matta had a line of black running under her left eye to her ear.

Elog saw the dark line and guessed she'd swept the hair falling across her face with a blackened hand, since there was soot on her hand. "Tatta," he said quietly, using his childhood name for her, "I feel part of me is lost. I worry. What if Elka fails to return?"

"She will return this time, Elog," she reassured him, "but there will come a time when she leaves and will not return. That is long from now. Do not spend time thinking on it. Nothing is forever."

Geol, from the back of the shelter raised his eyebrows. He had never considered that someday Elka would leave and fail to return. He wondered what his wife meant, but she was talking to Elog, and he would not interrupt. His wife had his full attention.

"What do you mean, Tatta?" Elog asked, horrified that sometime in the future his twin would go and not return. Already he was thinking on it, as she'd warned him not to do.

"Elog, once born, you and Elka remained close, but your personal integrity and hers are separate just as your bodies are separate and different. Each of you has a wholeness of your own, though you feel part of each other. Truth is, you are not. There is a special closeness, but your integrity is separate. Do you understand? You have a path of your own, while she has one of hers." She looked at his face and deep into his eyes, though cataracts badly clouded her vision. She saw with eyes of the spirit with exceptional clarity.

Matta continued, "Her completeness in life is partly moving in the direction of yours and partly very different. You cannot control those things anymore than you can control the day that someone dies." Matta stared off into the distance and then returned. "When separated, if that person's spirit is part of your life, you have them with you always, even when they're gone temporarily or forever."

"Tatta, when someone dies at a distance, you don't know they're dead."

Matta looked at her young grandson through tired eyes. "Sometimes you do," she replied, "Sometimes they come to tell you. Sometimes you just feel it. It can come in a dream." She was silent for a long time. "Elog, death doesn't end life. It moves it from this world to the next, where you live in a spirit body. Death is not an end but beginning in a different world."

Elog sat very still looking at his hands. He finally looked up. "I heard the stories say what you just said, but it didn't really make sense to me. I see no openings to walk through to the next world."

"You don't see because you don't look, and your expectations are strange," his grandmother replied slowly after a brief space of time.

Elog sat up straight, paying close attention. Geol didn't move, scarcely breathed, as he, too, listened.

"The next time you are aware that someone dies, stay there. Don't run off fearfully. Watch the chest carefully with the eyes you'd use to see motion at a distance. Be quiet and respectful. When death occurs, you can see the spirit leave the body. It rises to the opening of the next life, and then it vanishes. But you can see it for moments after death. You can see it vanish. There is an opening that points the way to their destination. I think these openings are prepared by waiting spirits, just before someone dies. They're not there all the time. The spirit opening takes spirit. The spirit world knows our world. We barely know theirs."

"Did you ever try to touch it?" Elog asked, spellbound.

"Try what?"

"Putting your hand in a spirit opening to see your hand disappeared?" Elog replied.

"Elog!" Matta exclaimed and paused, "You don't tempt or play games with spirits. Most people don't expect to see such things after death or they fear the dead, so they don't see it and never know. It is a special farewell to watch a spirit leave. It lets us remove fear by knowing there really is a spirit world, and how we go there. It's not something to play with or tempt. You do not ever want a spirit mad at you."

Geol listened intently, not moving. His wife had so many things to share, if only he'd ask. Rarely did he ever wonder about the things she knew. He was fascinated this time.

"And Elka is not harmed?"

"No, Grandson, Elka is fine. I know. She experiences aloneness. It is new to her."

Elog smiled for the first time that day. His heart was lightened. He believed her.

"I've never been alone," Elog said. Elka was doing something separate from him, and he was not sharing it. That bothered him somehow.

"Now go, Elog, stretch yourself—not someone else—yourself. Contribute to the clan's integrity today."

Suddenly, Elog had a feeling come over him, an understanding. He must grow separate from Elka, he had his own completeness to achieve. She wasn't hesitating to grow separate from him. She even knew what it was to feel alone. He had to stretch to become a man separate from his sister. That must have been what his father meant, but he had understood only as a child. He felt stretched already. Stretched in understanding that words had meaning sometimes beyond what first came to his thoughts. Like digging a hole in sand, he thought, and digging deeper there was a layer of clay. Still the same hole, only deeper with different substance. He would not forget. He resolved to listen more carefully in the future.

Elog picked up his spear and instantly saw his uncles, Jin and Lum. Lum invited him to hunt. They would hunt deer together until dusk. And that, he already understood, would not only be a contribution to clan integrity but also an opportunity to stretch himself apart and grow differently from Elka. Elog stood a little straighter, a little closer to manhood.

Abu and Sum had left as soon as Dal had handed Abu the provisions for their run. They jogged off and soon afterwards broke into a full run, as if they were going from one place to another quickly, though not at emergency speed. Unlike Elka, they knew the route to the area where they expected to find the carcass.

Back at the small river, Elka stared appraisingly at the tree after looking around herself. She decided the safest place to sleep that night would be in the tree. The expanse of the land that thrilled her on her arrival, suddenly gave her a feeling of vulnerability as the sun began its descent. Elka realized predators might seize her with ease on land. She noticed a part of the tree with strong branches that seemed ideal for her to use as a bed. She'd make herself a place to sleep in the tree. There was plenty of light left to the day, but she wanted to be ready.

Elka went to the river and gathered sedges to use to soften the place she'd sleep. She had used her belt to tie around the armload of sedges to help bring them with her up the tree. They were slippery and she had about as many on the ground as in the tree. Elka had to make three trips up the tree with her burdens to make the tree barely comfortable. With much daylight before sunset she was established in the tree, feeling only a small bit less vulnerable. Suddenly, Elka realized she was thirsty, so she climbed down, went to drink more water, and returned.

She tried to cover herself with some of the sedges for warmth but the effect was poor. She realized to be effective she would have had to weave them. She began to understand some things she'd seen all her life but never knew the thinking behind it. Weaving sedges was one. To use them for warmth, they had to be brought together tighter to keep them from slipping away. Air holes needed to be tighter.

There were about eight fingers of light left. Elka ran to the river, grabbed plenty of sedges, returned to do some fast, crude weaving, and climbed the tree with her product. She tried it out. The effect of her covering was slightly better, but she still felt chilled from below. She noticed that the roots of one of the sedges was dripping cold water on her foot. She tried to avoid it, being partly successful, since there were many roots. In the distance a wolf called. It was answered by another wolf seemingly coming from a distant place. Elka returned to gather more sedges. Her covering would become her undercover, and she'd make a better covering by weaving tighter.

Bugs began to make their night noises. Some mosquitoes lit upon her exposed skin and bit. Elka wondered whether she would sleep.

Abu and Sum had run hard and were nearing the tree where they'd make their turn to the north. It was over the next hill. They slowed. Finally, they stopped. As they cooled they lowered themselves to the ground, bending their knees, and resting their butts on their heels. Fully cooled, Abu pulled out his water bag and drank. Sum did the same.

"Good run," Abu said to cut the silence more than communicate.

"Yes," Sum agreed for the same reason. "The tree should be over the next hill."

"We still have some light left," Abu said quietly.

"I hope we see her," Sum said after another deep drink of water. "Ready?" he asked after tying off his water skin.

Abu stood and the two jogged off towards the west.

Soon the tree appeared against the horizon. They slowed, both noticing a lump in the center of the tree that looked abnormal.

"That her?" Sum asked, hopeful.

"Could be," Abu said, also hopeful. "Could also be a big cat."

"I'd rather not think about that." Sum laughed a little nervously.

They sped up.

Elka saw something on the horizon moving steadily towards her. She was frightened and had crouched ball-like in the tree. As the shape came closer, she could see it was two people. That gave her hope and fear all at the same time, since she had no way to know who they might be.

When the men reached her, she recognized them before they were certain she was Elka, since she had the advantage of what little light from the sinking sun there was.

"Come down here at once," Abu demanded.

Once she stood before him he grabbed her by the braid and brought her face close to his chest. "Explain yourself!"

"You're hurting me," she said in agony. The pain from having her hair pulled was making it hard for her to think. Elka had never received any pain from her father. She didn't understand. Raising her hands toward the root of the braid didn't help. She couldn't move her father's hand. Standing on first one foot and then another didn't help, but it seemed automatic.

"I said, explain yourself!" Abu made his voice gruff, yanking the braid so she had to look at his face. "Geol said we were not going here, until he was ready."

"Father, you are really hurting me," Elka complained, tears forming and running freely down her face.

Abu didn't have any desire to hurt her, but he'd been warned to be firm, to discipline his wayward girl. He held the braid tight and slapped her.

Elka wept. She was in pain but worse was the pain came from her father, now a stranger, who treated her unkindly. From someone who loved her, it was wholly confusing.

Abu did not loosen his grip on the braid. Sum wondered what had possessed Abu, but it was his right to discipline his daughter, so Sum maintained silence. It bothered him though, and he turned to avoid seeing it.

"Grandfather said no one was to go there to gather material for tools, until he was ready," she replied, tears still falling. "I didn't go to gather tools but rather to look to see what manner of beast died. I just wanted to know what died. It was a chance to do something different."

"That's men's scout work, not girl's work," Sum said, adding back his presence. The eagle feather Sum wore on his braid seemed about to fall, but Elka didn't mention it.

"True," Abu supported Sum. "You are not supposed to wander off from home. You had been forbidden to come here."

"But I didn't come here to gather tool-making material," she protested, her hands lightly placed around her father's on her head, tears falling. He jerked her head toward his face again.

"You disobeyed your grandfather," he insisted.

"I didn't know what I did was disobedience, Father, truly. Please, turn loose my braid."

"What have you eaten?" Abu asked his daughter, completely missing the realization that he'd just told his son to stretch himself, while he expected his daughter to restrict herself by staying close to home. Abu looked at his daughter's tears. Hol had impressed on him to be firm, but Elka's tears were hitting him hard.

"Father, please free my hair, It hurts so bad."

Abu loosened his grip but did not let her go. Elka was aware, but it didn't decrease the pain she felt.

"What I ate. . . . I ate three yellow lotus flowers and three crayfish," she told her father. "I also had some chickweed that grows over there," she pointed to the place.

Abu made a sound as if to acknowledge but without approval or disapproval. Inwardly he was proud of her. Catching crayfish in such a tiny river with a sandy bottom was not easy. He did not turn loose of her braid.

"Sit," he commanded and shoved her to the ground by the braid.

She was agonizing over the treatment, still confused over having done anything wrong. Finally, Abu released the braid.

Abu really wanted to see the carcass. He held his hand at arm's length, fingers horizontal to the ground between the sun and his eyes. He estimated they had plenty of time to reach the carcass in some light. His hunger won out. They would eat and then go to see the carcass.

He pulled out of his backpack a bag he carried. Sum had begun a small fire in a depression he scooped out in the sand, and they surrounded it. Abu pulled out three sticks and a wrapped package of smoked deer. He stuck a piece of deer meat on Elka's stick and handed it to her.

She wanted to weep for joy, but instead, quite dry eyed, she said, "Thank you, Father. Thank you, deer." She hovered her meat over the flame to warm it, relieved that it seemed her father was more himself.

Abu nodded. He laid the provisions bag open between Sum and himself. Sum found his dangling eagle feather and stuck it firmly into his braid. Each speared some meat and held it above the fire. The scent was wonderful and all three were salivating profusely, long before they began to eat.

"Until I tell you different, you don't have permission to leave the home camp again. Even to go to the lake. You must ask every time you want to be beyond sight of the camp. The hill's flat top is your limit. Understand?"

"Yes." Elka was not happy at all with this restriction, but she listened and realized this was serious. She had come close to breaking her individual integrity. She wasn't exactly certain how, but she knew it was serious.

"You were frightened when you sought the tree for a bed—right?"

"Yes, Father," she said, wondering how he knew.

"Suddenly, it wasn't great freedom to be alone—right?"

"Yes."

"Starting to get cold?"

"Yes."

Abu handed her another piece of meat, then leaned over and wrapped her rabbit cape with tie around her shoulders. Dal had put the cape in the bag without asking, knowing Elka'd need it. Abu felt it when he reached for the meat in his backpack.

"Thank you," she whispered. Elka wanted to cry, but held back her tears. She concentrated on warming and eating the meat. When she finished, she tied the cape so it wouldn't slip off. Carefully she pulled her braid so it would lie atop the cape instead of being covered by it. Moving the braid caused her to wince. There was still pain where her father had held it so tight and jerked her around with it.

"Thank your mother," Abu said a bit louder.

"Thank you, Mother."

The very idea of having to remain at camp within visual distance was beginning to enter her dark thoughts. Elka was horrified at the confinement. To leave it she must ask permission. What if, she wondered, her father were on a hunting trip? She already sensed the answer. He did his thinking tightly. She was far looser. After all, Geol had not said they couldn't go to the carcass site for reasons other than gathering supplies for tools. Elka worried over what her life would become with such restrictions. She felt close to despair.

Sum and Abu put their things away. Sum extinguished the fire.

"As long as we're here, we might as well look at the carcass, since Geol will, no doubt, ask us about it."

Sum nodded. He felt awkward going to the site, but he was definitely interested. Sum was eager to return to this place soon with Geol. He had need of additional spoons, an adze, and blades. He wanted to have some sharper points to attach to his spear. He'd also like to have a drill. He would not, however, touch anything on the carcass, for, he knew, Geol would not approve.

Elka looked at her father. He and Sum had come to find her, of that she was convinced. They found her. She suspected he was as curious as she was, but shifted it off onto Geol. Her father had told her that coming here to see the carcass was disobedience to Geol. She had cold shivers. Claiming that Geol would ask about the carcass was a lie, wasn't it? Her father had no idea what Geol would ask. She assumed her father wanted to see the carcass as much as she did.

The members of the clan had been carefully taught to tell things exactly the way they were. No lies were ever permitted. Slightly shading something away from truth was a lie. To lie was to break personal integrity. If personal integrity was fully broken, people were banished from the clan. They had to leave quickly or they could be killed. They were taught the clan cannot survive without personal and clan integrity. She shuddered. She'd seen her father treat her as he never had, as a mean-spirited stranger might treat her. She'd never known her father to lie or shade things differently from what they were. The confusion was overwhelming.

Had she just witnessed personal integrity broken? She would not ask. She would remain silent about her thoughts and confusion. There was something amiss here, and she was uncertain. Maybe, she hoped, her guess that he was using Geol to satisfy his curiosity was an error. She let the thoughts go. She could prove nothing.

Picking up water pouches, the two men went to the little river to fill the bags. They returned quickly. Elka's father grabbed her wrist, and they began to jog. Elka felt ridiculous being led like a little child, she resented it, but she did not fight back. She didn't know what would happen if she fought back, and she didn't want her braid grabbed again.

The jog speed increased to a gentle run. Elka was able to keep the pace. They ran for quite some time. More and more trees began to appear to the west and east, though fewer to the east. They went up and down small hills and a lot of uneven ground. The site was beyond where Elka expected to find it. A slight strange odor wafted by from time to time.

"We're getting close," Sum shouted out. "There it is!"

Abu shoved Elka to the side on the little rise beyond reach of the carcass. "Stay here," he said firmly. Elka was so undone that she would do nothing but obey her father, quickly and completely. She stood as still as a great-blue-heron fishing. She stared at her father. Abu had complete authority to control her, she knew. That was so the clan might have clan integrity.

It was one of the rules. The man ruled his home. He was required to do so. Normally, however, the only person who took that rule to any length was Hol in his treatment of his wife. The way Abu was acting, Elka thought he was furious with her. She was fearful of making any move, even if her nose itched, as it did at that moment. She feared he might treat her as Hol treated Koa. She wiggled her nose and kept her arms at her side. She'd never been afraid of her father. She was now. She did not know he'd talked to Hol, before he left on this search.

Without moving, Elka looked at the rotting carcass in the dim light. It was mostly eaten, but enough remained that it still smelled bad—and peculiar.

"What's that strange odor?" Sum asked.

"No idea," Abu replied, pointing to the ground, looking at Elka. Elka sat. Her father nodded. She felt relieved that she'd understood his hand signal.

Sum approached the rotting carcass. There were no large scavengers present. He and Abu circled the great beast's remains. They looked at each other with blank looks. They knew it smelled a bit different, but they could make no sense of it. The broken tusk dangled from its place. Sum touched the dangling tusk with the tip of his spear, and it fell to the ground, tip first. For a moment it stood upright in the sand far longer than they expected, and, then, the tusk tip rolled to its side. The two men laughed as if it were the funniest thing they ever saw.

Elka had reached into her little bag where she kept the mastodon tooth cutting tool. She unwrapped the small, smooth rock she held. About the size of her thumb, the stone was of turquoise and gold. It had been rubbed so many times that it was smooth and soft in her hand. She thought of it as the shape of a bird. It comforted her in times of confusion or trouble. The present was such a time. She had not been permitted to approach the carcass—not that she desired to do so, and it was hard to see in the dark. The tiny stone brought her comfort while she waited. It seemed with the stone held tight in her hand that she could fly with the birds, way high above all the land, to see where people could go, if only they had the desire. She put the stone back in the piece of leather that protected it, dropped it into her pouch, and tied the pouch tight to the strip of leather that tied at the waist around her tunic.

After some time of examining the carcass, the men turned to leave.

Elka looked up at Abu. "Will we be sleeping here? It doesn't smell good."

Both men laughed.

Abu reached for her hand. "We run home. Very little sleep this night for us."

Elka remembered the distance she'd run. She was slightly dispirited, but she was aware that she'd brought this on herself. Elog, she remembered, tried to warn her. She would not complain.

A short way into the run, Sum noticed shapes on a hill on the horizon. He shouted a sound and Abu looked his way. Sum pointed. Abu saw the silhouettes of lions. He was glad there was as much distance between them as there was and that they were moving further distant from them. Otherwise, they might be viewed as targets for predation.

The night was cool. Running kept them plenty warm. The rabbit skin cape Elka wore flew behind her.

They began at a jog, then broke into a run. They reduced their normal speed somewhat to accommodate Elka, but often forgot, leaving her gasping for air with legs that screamed in pain. At times she fell, with Abu dragging her by the wrist, scraping her leg on the land. It was without any intent to harm her, it was just a long distance to cover and the men occasionally travelled faster than she could hope to run. At such times, Abu helped her up and they continued on, a little slower. After a few falls, Sum held her other wrist, so if she fell, she wouldn't be dragged to a stop.

As they ran, suddenly from the corner of her eye, Elka noticed something running with them to her father's right side. She had no breath for shouting, so she shook her arm as wildly as she could. Finally, he realized what was happening and slowed. She pointed with her gaze, terrified, to his right. He looked and, staring into his eyes, he saw a huge gray colored wolf. He halted, pushed Elka behind him, and attended to his spear. The wolf, that had been running with them, lay down and whined. Sum was confused by Abu's hesitation to kill the wolf.

Abu didn't know what to make of the wolf. He didn't feel right to spear a wolf who lay at his feet whining. The wolf, tail between its legs again, walked off, returned, whined, then walked off again, looking back.

"Does it want us to follow?" Elka asked.

They started to continue the run home, but the wolf, tail low, leaped in front of them. Finally, Abu had just enough curiosity to stop. He began to follow the wolf, wondering at his own stupidity. Could this be an ambush by wolves? It wasn't characteristic of their behavior to set up such an ambush. None of this was characteristic. They reached a wash where scrub trees grew, and in the light of the full moon, they could see a man lying there, apparently not conscious. Sum went to the man and found he was living. He had a gash on his head and side. The wolf lay beside the man.

"Astounding," Sum said, expressing their collective thoughts. They found it incomprehensible that a wolf led them to a wounded man.

The man roused. "I am Acconomaku, wanderer, teller of tales, traveler to many far distant places." His head dropped back down and he grimaced. He spoke a little differently, but his words were entirely understandable.

Sum said, "I remember you. A few years ago, you stayed with us a while."

He and Abu knew he was from a tribe far off to their east, across mountains and a big river. They had seen him long ago. He traveled from place to place, sharing stories of other people. The man needed help. The wolf lay beside him, not moving anything but its eyes.

Abu reached out to examine the man's wound, and the wolf began to raise its upper lip, thought better of it, and remained motionless. Acconomaku noticed.

"Good, Teera," the man mumbled. The wolf listened with its ears up, and then laid its ears back against its head, silent, still, and guarding with intensity. Elka was startled. The wolf had a name! It responded almost as if it understood the man.

"This is bad. Before the wound threatens his integrity, if it hasn't already, we must get him back to the clan. Sum, will you run? Elka will remain here with me." Abu was concerned. "Ask Jin to create a shelter for the man and this wolf. Warn all to keep away from the wolf. No screaming when they see the wolf. Return with a stretcher."

Without a word, Sum began to run. He was swift in his eagerness to help the injured man. He was, he knew, only two great hills away from home. There was no Elka to slow him down. He ran with all the speed he could. This was emergency running in his mind.

Abu, kneeling beside Acconomaku's mid-section, took off his shoulder bag and pulled out his water pouch. He offered the man some water. The man's gratitude was clear. Over time he consumed a lot of water slowly, the quantity surprising Abu.

Elka was fascinated by the wolf. She had been warned never to stare into the eyes of a wolf, so she glanced at the animal with her lashes down, and only obliquely. The idea of a wolf companion drew her interest as nothing had ever done. Could people really communicate with animals? She'd seen the man tell the wolf that lowering its lips from a snarl was good. The wolf seemed to understand.

Elka knew Matta talked to animals, but no one thought they understood each other. They laughed about her doing it. There was so much Elka wanted to know. Matta had healed animals that continued to come to her after returning to their lives, but still Elka found real communication hard to accept. Her life had taught her such things were the source of laughter, not to be taken seriously. To believe it, she had to reject what she'd been taught by elders.

The girl continued watching. The man, she saw clearly, had watched the wolf raise its lips in warning and then drop them. He understood the wolf, and the wolf seemed to understand his comment of "Good, Teera." It had not snarled or raised its lips again. Elka earnestly entertained the idea for the first time that communication between people and animals might be possible. She was squatting near the man's shoulder and she squeezed her hands tighter on her knees. If communication were possible, she wanted to learn how. It would be a wonderful thing to know.

The wolf knew she was being watched. The wolf was as curious about the girl as Elka was about the wolf. The wolf knew Elka was female and the others were male by scent.

Often, Teera heard the call of the wild wolves, and sometimes she answered, but mostly she lay at the man's feet quiet with maybe a tiny almost audible whine, her eyes searching the cave opening to see whether a wolf might appear. She was wolf, she knew, but she was loyal to the man, since he saved her when her wolves deserted her.

Teera had been close to death when the man brought her into his cave and cleaned her wound. She was still young then, just weaned. She had fallen down a hill and rocks had beaten her body. Her leg, cut by a sharp rock down to the bone, was painful. The man, Acconomaku, took hairs from his head and with his bone needle, he sewed the skin together over the bone. The man kept it clean, put honey on it, and told her not to lick it. He wrapped it in leather, pulling it together to get the skin to connect again to skin. He watched her. From time to time he opened the leather, cleaned the wound, put more honey and herbs on the wound, and rewrapped it. He fed her and brought her water while she was too weak to move.

Acconomaku stroked her side and spoke gently to her. A few times a day he took her legs and moved them as legs are supposed to move. He repeated the movements gently and for quite some time, telling her, as if she could understand, that she must keep moving so her legs would work. She did not understand every word, but she understood enough to know the man tried to help. As she healed, she became deeply attached to the man.

The wolf had not learned what young wolves learn from their mothers. She had learned instead to trust the man. He named her Teera, Little One. She didn't understand the meaning but knew when he said Teera, he meant her and only her. He taught her to hunt with him. She knew a few of his words. Teera would herd the prey to him on the hunt. He would spear it and share. As long as she understood what he wanted, she did his bidding. Sometimes, she did it without his guidance, knowing what he would want.

In time Sum returned with Lum. They opened the stretcher, and, as gently as possible, they placed the man on it.

Lum looked at the pained face of the man, "Who are you?" he asked.

"Acconomaku," the man said quietly. "I am traveler and teller of tales."

"I remember you," Lum said. "You looked familiar. Many years ago, you visited. Life has treated you well, until this," he added.

Acconomaku smiled weakly.

The men lifted the stretcher, Abu took Elka's wrist and they walked briskly towards home. The wolf trotted beside the stretcher, her eyes frequently checking Acconomaku's condition.

Arrival at home was unusual. The people were subdued in the presence of the wolf. They took Acconomaku to the shelter Jin had provided at the edge of the forest. It was part of their home area, but a little off towards the woods. Jin had tried to keep the wolf at a distance without making it terribly obvious. The bed arranged for Acconomaku was soft and the man was grateful. The wolf went to the far back of the shelter to be on Acconomaku's uninjured side to guard. It was night, but all the people were wide awake to attend the arrival of the small group.

Matta arrived and spoke very quietly to the man. She glanced at the wolf and the animal sensed that Matta would care for Acconomaku. It was instantaneous understanding. She nodded at the wolf. She pushed the deerskin aside and looked at the wound.

"No treatment for some time," she remarked.

"I lost consciousness," he tried to explain. "Don't know for how long. Teera watched over me. She licked the wound."

"You hurt anywhere?" she asked, trying to assess the damage to the man.

"My legs have little feeling. That is troubling. I am a traveler."

"I remember," Matta said very quietly.

As gently as possible Matta turned the man on his side to face the wolf. Then, she returned him to his back.

"You have much swelling. Maybe things will be better, when swelling goes down," she said plainly. "Wiggle your feet."

Acconomaku wiggled his feet.

"They work," she told him. "Good sign."

"What happened to you?" She began to wash the wound on his side. She motioned to Abu to raise his chest so she could slip the long wide strip of leather under him. It would hold poultices against the wound. The wolf became alarmed, but remained still. The wolf did move its paws out of Matta's way as she tugged on the leather band. Matta washed the wound again and smoothed a poultice over it. She pulled the wrap up and through slits, she poked a wooden spike to hold the leather in place, so it in turn would hold the poultice.

Acconomaku winced. "I'm not sure. A saber-toothed cat sprang up from tall grass, surprising me, and I think I fell into the wash, where your people found me. When I came back to this world, my wolf was by my side and there was no cat anywhere I could see. I realized I hurt and could not move for the pain of it."

"We will care for you. You may return to normal or not. It's up to the level of the integrity of your body. You need to sleep." Matta patted his shoulder and departed.

Using her hand signals, she indicated to the people to return to their sleep. There was nothing more to do.

Elog sought out Elka. He was eager to tell of his hunting achievement in her absence, but when he saw her, he noticed she was different. Something had happened to her. He put his arm around her shoulders and led her off to their shelter. He would wait until later to talk. She seemed exhausted. In the torch light he could see one side of her face was red. He wondered what happened. He felt certain she'd explain all later. They always shared everything. He helped her lie down and covered her legs gently with a soft deer skin and pulled a piece of furry, somewhat moth-eaten bear hide over her shoulders down to her knees. He curled up on his side next to her and put his arm around her. His arm enjoyed the softness of the fur on the skin he'd used as cover for her. Either she had already drifted to sleep, or she just didn't want to talk. He respected her and let himself drift back to sleep.

Hol walked up to Abu and shoved him hard, using his stiff fingers with their broken nails as a tool to inflict

61

pain on his brother. "What possessed you to defile the integrity of our clan with this animal?" Hol hissed.

Abu noticed Hol's nails had drawn blood on his shoulder. Breaking skin was an invitation to breaking integrity. Infection could set in. Abu didn't hesitate, he attacked Hol. In a flash he had his brother on the ground in a chokehold. Hol could barely breathe.

"First thing with the light of day," Abu said more calmly than he felt, "you will file down those nails to the nail bed. I will check to be sure you have. If you ever draw my blood again, you will be banished from the clan. Is that clear?"

Hol failed to respond. Abu applied more pressure. Hol said, "Yes."

Abu let him get up.

Hol shook himself after regaining his feet. He brushed off his skirt. He hoped not many had seen the incident. Geol had, however, seen and heard the brothers. He strode over and held Hol by the upper arms, glaring into his middle child's face. "Your brother gave you one more chance. I was on my way here to exile you from camp. You are lacking in integrity. One more incident from you and you're out. Is that clear?"

Hol nodded. He felt the treatment was unfair, but then, he felt, people always treated him unfairly. He wasn't as big, strong, or attractive as Abu. He wasn't the hunter his brother, Sum, was, but he was part of the clan, and they should treat him equally. In some ways, he was convinced, he was better than his brothers. He was sure he was much smarter and cleverer. On hunts he could often spot prey others failed to see. Where was the respect he deserved? In a huff he returned to his wife, Koa, in their shelter. She would calm him. She was a good woman.

There was no instant sleep. There was much to murmur about as the members of the clan lay in their beds. Only slowly did the little clan return to sleep. Stars continued their trek in the world above, soon to be joined by the dawning sun and a new day.

PART TWO

Rain was falling. It was generally welcome in this drought. Matta could hear it bounce from the cover of vegetation onto the aging skins that made their shelter's interior. She reached for Geol and discovered he'd already risen. She thought they might need to increase the evergreen boughs atop their inner shelter. They had recently been replaced, she knew, so maybe just adding to them would provide greater protection against rain until the weather improved. Then, they could use some of the waxy castoreum from beavers to treat the leather, making it waterproof. She didn't want a path for water to leak through the leather into the shelter. She had too many supplies for treating the clan, supplies water would ruin. Rain must stay outside the shelter. It was not a hard rain but hard enough to bounce on the top of the shelter skins in a few places. It would make mud on the ground. Matta had little appreciation for mud except as a topical application for sprains to reduce swelling or a pain support in cases of spider or insect bites. Clay was better for that purpose, she thought.

Matta had slept deeply after being awakened in the night for the traveler. She was not surprised Acconomaku had a wolf companion. He was a man who knew spirits. Many could reach the spirit of animals and communicate through that means. It wasn't difficult. What was hard was trying to explain that to others, others in whom spiritual life barely breathed, if it lived at all. Matta smiled.

She gazed foggily about the shelter, her cataracts making sight difficult. She went to her medicine storage with a piece of leather. She had ground substances that she'd mix to make a poultice for Acconomaku's wounds. She sniffed and then took mesquite, desert sage, plantain, and yarrow and pinched the proper amounts of ground material onto the leather. Her nose for these things told her more than her eyes. Matta took her container of globe mallow and stored all the rest. She mixed the ground herbs with honey in a small stone bowl. Matta took a fresh piece of prickly pear cactus from a basket, slit it, and scraped some of the inner material into the bowl. She had enough to make a good poultice for the traveler's wounds. With her sharp knife, she mixed the materials together thoroughly. Matta smelled it. She reached out for another pinch of sage and stirred it into the mixture. She wiped her knife on a piece of leather.

"That'll do it," she said to no one but herself.

She left her shelter with the poultice bowl and the container of globe mallow, after draping a deer skin over her head and shoulders. She didn't like wet hair. She headed to the shelter where the traveler would lie, arriving not too wet. The traveler was alone. While she hung her head covering on a stunted branch, she wondered whether the wolf frightened people, those who otherwise might stop to speak to the man. She noticed that Jin had selected well the site where the shelter stood. The floor was completely dry. She smiled a tiny smile.

"It's a good rainy morning," she said flatly.

"Yes," Acconomaku agreed.

Matta pulled the spike from the wrap and examined the wound.

"Well, Acconomaku, the wound does not look any different. Your integrity must be solid. There's not even a bad odor. It needs to tie together. I will sew it together. Maybe this afternoon. Can you pull some long hairs from your head?

"If I must," he replied with a smile. "I'll have them ready for you when you return."

"Good. Your own hair is best for this, as you know."

"Yes."

Matta took a soft piece of leather hanging in the shelter and held it outside the shelter. She pulled down the leather roof gently, making water run into the leather, soaking it. She gently squeezed the leather piece and then used it to wash the man's side and head wounds.

"Has Geol stopped by?" she asked as she worked. Geol was supposed to bring the man something into which he could relieve himself, as well as a water bag and help drinking water, if needed.

"He did. It appears you've thought of everything, Matta," the man said.

"Well, what I don't know how to do—is to make it so people will visit without fear of the wolf."

She began to apply the poultice.

"That's Teera," he assured her.

"Teera? You mean Young or Little One in the language of those far to the east?"

"Yes. When, I found her she was just a pup. She'd been injured badly. I had to take care of her for a long time."

"Her pack had left her?" Matta was shocked.

"She would have stopped their travel for moons, injured as she was, so, yes, they left her."

"How sad," she whispered. She looked at Teera. "You were lucky Acconomaku found you, Teera."

The wolf raised her head and ears. Her two front paws stretched, touching the man's side. The wolf looked right at Matta, making the tiniest sound.

Matta smiled. "Treat him well, Teera," she said reaching out and touching the wolf on her shoulder. The wolf made the tiny sound again, lowering her head to her paws.

"What's that?" Acconomaku asked Matta.

"Globe mallow," she replied, "It is like a wet glue that keeps the wound from getting dirty. I like it"

"Interesting," he told her. It was a plant he didn't know.

After wrapping Acconomaku's head and side wounds, Matta put on her head covering and left.

Elka was drawn to the man and wolf. She arrived shortly after Matta left. She kneeled beside him.

"I'm Elka," she introduced herself, water dripping from her hand onto his arm.

"I'm Acconomaku," he returned. "You were with the men who found me."

"Yes. It was Teera who told us where you were. She didn't want us to pass by and not find you."

Acconomaku pulled up his head and looked at Teera. He reached out with his left hand and stroked the part of Teera's back he could reach.

"She's a wonderful companion," he said.

"Teera seems to understand you," Elka said, barely controlling her hunger to know about human-wolf communication.

"You want to know if we make sense communicating to each other?"

Elka nodded.

Acconomaku looked carefully at the young girl. She was too thin, but some day she would be beautiful. Her eyes were extraordinary, her smile arresting. She must be mischievous, he thought, because it appeared she'd been slapped on the cheek. Her legs were scraped on the sides. Her wrists were bruised. They were out at night. Acconomaku could piece the scene together. Two adult males running home with a young girl between them. She tried to keep up, but had trouble. Had they stolen her? Had she run off from home? He reasoned the latter or she'd be restrained now. Poor little one, he thought. And, he was aware, she must be alive spiritually. A rarity, he considered, in a world where vital spirit appeared to be dying out.

"You saw us communicate down at the wash, didn't you?" he asked.

"Yes."

"Do you not trust what you see and hear?"

"I know Matta talks to animals. The clan laughs behind her back, saying she thinks she's communicating, but she's only saying words they don't understand. The people laugh at her." Elka was horrified that so much had come from her mouth, and she quickly covered her mouth with her hands.

"What if I told you, they're communicating spiritually?"

"How can that be?" she asked, completely surprised.

"All living things have spirits. Some think rocks and rivers and other non-living things have spirits, too. There is a language for living things to speak to each other. There is also a spirit language where spirits can speak to spirits."

Elka's mouth hung open. She had never considered such a thing.

"How, then, did your father realize Teera wanted him to follow?"

"I watched her lying at his feet, whining. She'd get up and walk toward you, looking back. She'd get up and walk toward you. I asked my father if the wolf was trying to get him to follow."

"So, you understood the spiritual request for help from Teera, and you spoke it to your father in people-to-people language. Isn't that how it happened?"

"But I didn't hear her in my spirit say those things."

"Your spirit ears are not the same as the ears on the side of your head. Can you tell me you didn't *know* down deep inside exactly what Teera wanted?"

"Acconomaku, I thought I did, but I wasn't certain. That's why I asked my father."

"Your father does not have a sensitive spirit like your grandmother. Yours is far stronger than his. I'm not sure at all that your father has a live spirit. His may be sleeping."

"How do you know that?' Elka was off centered by what she was hearing.

"Which one of you understood Teera?"

"I guessed at what she wanted."

"How do you know you guessed, and didn't actually hear her spirit speak to your spirit, so you could put it in your language?"

"That's how it works?"

"Until you do it frequently. Then the middle part takes less time and is almost not there."

"Then, they can understand us, even when we're not talking to them?"

"Not necessarily. A strange bird might see you at a tree bent over and weeping. It doesn't know whether you're angry, sad, sick, or what. The bird would know instantly that something was abnormal. If interested, it would observe you from a distance. It would not try to comfort you as Teera does with me now. Teera knows me for many days. She trusts me. Trust is part of the spiritual communication. If you differ from what they expect from you, it can destroy their trust. Destroy trust, and communication dies." Acconomaku took a sip of water.

He continued, "Trust breaks down just like integrity breaks down, if a person lies or steals. The person is no longer the person they were before lying or stealing. Animals rely on your constant integrity to trust you, just like people do, maybe even more. Teera trusts me wholly right now. If I yelled at her, it would frighten her. She would always have a doubt lingering that I might yell at her again. She would not know what to expect to come with that yelling. Animals don't change the way they act. We could learn from them."

"Then when I went on my long run yesterday to see the carcass of the mastodon, my clan was frightened, because it was not something they'd expect me to do? I didn't want to frighten anyone."

Acconomaku stifled his smile.

"You took off that far away to see a dead mastodon?"

"Well, we knew it was a carcass, a big one. We could see many dead-eater birds from here. They were the big dead-eater birds. Geol didn't want to gather tool-making bones until he was ready. We couldn't go for tool-making supplies until he was ready, so I thought it was permitted to go for other reasons. I was just curious."

"Many living things die every day because of curiosity, Little Girl," he said slowly, rising for a moment to sip some water.

"Did it not occur to you that the trip was too long?"

"No. I decided to run. I'm a fast runner. I thought I could go there and be home before dark. Now, I know how wrong I was."

"There is a clan near the ocean that is desperate for women. If they had found you, believe me, they would have run off with you, and your family would never have seen you again. You'd be used as a woman, though you're not ready yet. Do you understand?"

"That would be terrible," Elka replied shocked. "Have they no integrity?" She put her hands to her knees, and, almost stood up, as though people from the coast were coming her way. Then, she relaxed.

"In such cases, people throw away integrity to satisfy need."

"Integrity is forever," she said, repeating what she'd been taught.

"You might have lost yours yesterday and entered your dead forever."

"How?" For Elka, his words were one shock after another.

"A few prides of lions are out there searching for food. I saw them. There are also some bison, and I saw a bear a few days ago. I walk with a wolf. Few predators are willing to stand against a fully grown human and wolf. Against a girl alone out there. You wouldn't last long. They wouldn't get much meat off you, but they'd get you, if they saw or smelled you."

"So, that's why my father was angry?"

"Well, that and by having to go after you, you put their lives at risk also. That would be my thought."

"Oh, I'm so sorry." That idea had never crossed her mind. Of course, she had expected to be home before night.

"You're telling the wrong person that, Elka. You should be telling your father. You showed poor thinking, if any thinking at all. You're a lot smarter than that."

"Hello, Acconomaku," Elog said as he approached the shelter. He looked at the wolf, not the man. "Will the wolf bite?"

"If you tried to hurt me, she might kill you," the man replied with a grin, "but for you just to come here to talk, no, she won't hurt you. She has one job. Protect me. That's it."

"Oh," Elog stammered. "Uh, Elka, Father wants to see you—now."

Elka stood, looked at Acconomaku and said, "Thank you. You have given me so much to think on."

She hurried toward her home shelter next to Geol and Matta's. Once inside her eyes had to accustom to the darkness. Her father sat on his sleeping place. In an unusual gesture, Elka threw herself down on the ground before him.

"Father, I am so very, very sorry. Yesterday, I failed to think. I didn't remember that the place was so far. I never thought of the predators out there. It never occurred to me that you'd have to search for me. There are lions, bears, and bison out there right now. I learned that from the storyteller. I put you and Sum at risk as well as myself. There is a clan near the ocean in desperate need of women who might have stolen me, if they'd seen me. Father, I am so sorry." She wept, clearly with an anguished spirit.

"Come here," he ordered.

She stood up, face thoroughly soaked. She didn't try to wipe the tears away. She went to him and stood right in front of him. He reached up with his open hand and wiped the tears to her hairline.

"You learned something?"

"Oh, yes."

"Now, learn something more. Listen carefully. Hol has wanted you for Barg. Nevermind," he waved off her visible anxiety. "I know you dislike Barg. Barg is like his father with a bit harder mean streak. If you ever leave home or do anything with as much lack of thought as yesterday, I will give you to Barg, even if you're not fully a woman. Understand?'

Elka had sucked in so much air as she listened to her father that she could do nothing but expel it all at once in a great cry. "No! You wouldn't do that."

"I trust that will keep you at home and not off doing something else equally stupid." Abu strung out the word stupid as if it tasted bad. "If you will not control yourself, I'm sure Barg will be delighted to spend the rest of his life doing just that."

Elka wrung her hands in front of her father. She was horrified. She fully expected some day to see Hol removed from the clan. His wife would have to go with him. An exile and wife, perhaps with children, would not likely survive. It had happened. A wife belonged to her husband. He could beat her, if he chose. She could not lift a hand against him, no matter what he did. To Elka it was unfair, hideously, mercilessly unfair.

She did not want ever to become some man's owned thing. She had felt that way a long time, having observed adults in the clan. She might consider Ranu. Ranu was from the Tip group in their clan; she was from Geol's. Tip and Geol were not related. To be forced to mate with another of Geol's group would be wrong. Barg was from Geol's group. A wrong her father considered doing against her. She trusted him to be serious; she believed him. He was changed, or she had just been given a glimpse of what he hid from others. She didn't know which. She was uncertain of what once she had found unquestionable. She wondered whether her father loved or hated her.

Elka had been close to Ranu since they were little. She thought they would end up together, but not one other person could she even consider. Ranu was kind and thoughtful. The others were always showing off. If she couldn't be with Ranu, she'd definitely run away so she could never be found. No man would treat her as Hol treated Koa.

Koa, who had been pretty and so happy, Elka'd been told, now went about with her head hung low, hunched over, frightened all the time, and never smiled. She didn't talk to other women or children. She was like someone dead responding to every stupid demand Hol made, and he demanded all day long every little thing one could imagine. Barg hunted. She did all the rest in their home. Hol's children feared him, for he would not hesitate to beat them. Hol's only contribution to the family was hunting, and he expected Barg and his wife to bleed the prey and tend to the butchering. His wife also had to tend to the skin and other parts of the animal to keep their supplies up to date. Most of the time, Koa was exhausted. If she didn't finish her jobs, she stayed awake until they were all done. Circles under her eyes were deep purple.

Matta and Geol kept an eye on Koa. They had decided if Hol put Koa's life at critical risk, Geol would intervene and banish Hol from the clan without Koa. Reorg and Pogu watched over Koa with Matta and Geol to detect anything that might be outright unacceptable. Pogu was convinced it had already passed the line of acceptable, but she was afraid to speak out. She couldn't discuss it with Sum, her husband, Matta and Geol's youngest son. The men, except for Geol, had no idea the women and Geol were watching over Koa.

Some of the men in the clan spoke to Hol about how he treated his wife. They explained how he had misinterpreted their rules. Hol wouldn't listen. Instead he accused them of being afraid of their wives—or jealous. There was no way to reach the man. The clan had provision for a husband to divorce his wife, but there was no way for a wife to divorce her husband.

Elka didn't know it, but long ago the women had concluded that their way to divorce was through poison, either by taking it themselves or giving it to the man. It was their secret, one they never dared to share. They alone had the keys to medicine. They alone knew which plants had a toxic quality, and how much was the toxic amount. That was their only recourse.

They all felt it was a wrong defense, but as they expressed it among themselves, they were trapped. When times grew desperate, women would do desperate things, and behind it all, they would join strong together. They had a sisterly integrity that kept them strong. They didn't hate men. They hated the distribution of power in such unequal ways. Often, they found ways around the inequality. Strong as the bond they shared, however, they had found no way to help Koa.

Elka remained standing before Abu. Suddenly and unexpectedly, he grabbed her arm and reached up under her tunic with his rough callused hand. The hand sought out her breasts. Elka was overwhelmed. This wasn't something for which she had ever been prepared. Abu discovered no growth there. He slid his hand roughly down belly to her pubic area to discover it was hairless. Elka tried desperately to pull away, but he held her tight by the arm and jerked her back, bruising her arm. Abu felt around her genitals roughly.

"Don't ever pull away from me again, or I will take you by the braid and hand you to Barg," he said through clenched teeth.

Elka wanted to scream. Her father had, she had been taught, rights to do whatever he wanted, so she tried to control herself, though she felt somehow inappropriately handled. Fathers didn't touch their daughters; mothers didn't touch their sons—there. Down deep inside she knew this was wrong, but she could find no support anywhere for her thoughts. She would have to be careful what she said and to whom. Her father's Barg threat hung heavy over her.

Elka's face was brilliant red. She was horrified, angry, and frustrated. No one had ever done that to her. His touch was rough. It reminded her of his pulling her braid. Her father looked hard at her. Finally, he released her arm.

"Are you holding back becoming woman? I was thinking you might be a boy."

She looked incredulous. "I wouldn't want to hold back, but if I did, I wouldn't know how, Father." Such a thought had never crossed her mind.

"You should be near woman now."

Elka had no idea what his concern was. Returning from sewing up Acconomaku's wound, Matta walked past Abu's shelter at the time this was happening. She stood outside to listen, and, then, she made some noise and stepped inside. She had heard Abu's words, though she had to guess what he was doing. She guessed he was being rough with Elka to assert power over her.

"What are you doing, my son?" she asked Abu.

"I'm wondering when Elka will be a woman." Matta was alarmed, but did not show it.

"Abu, that is a matter for women. She cannot control that part of her life. When the moon spirit decides she will be woman, she will be. Until then, leave it be. Some females don't become women until ten and six or seven full sets of seasons. It is not a decision for you to make. Leave it alone."

"I am man now, Mother. I do as I like. She can have a husband before she's a woman."

"No!" Matta was adamant, spitting out the words, horrified. "The moon spirit knows when she's ready, not you. Mess with your mother or spirits and you will find that doing what you like, when it wrongs another, brings broken integrity on your head," she said as she stomped out of Abu's shelter. Abu sat up straighter, as if in protest, but she frightened him all the same. She was closer to the spirits than any person in their clan.

Matta turned back. In a strong but quiet voice she added, as if knowing his thoughts, "And my son, the girl before you has as much spirit power as I do. There is no one in this clan who has more spirit power than she does. I know how to use it, while she is just learning. You'd be wise to consider that now and for the future. Do no wrong to her. Don't play power against her. The spirits will not like it. They will tell me." She left.

Elka was stunned. Abu dropped her arm as if it burned his fingers.

"You may go," Abu said to Elka. He added, "The clan built on this flat hill. Do not step one step outside the boundary of this hilltop without my permission. Only my permission. No one can tell you for me. Permission to leave this land must come from my mouth."

"I will obey you, Father," Elka said.

Elka wanted to crawl into her bed to sleep, but her father was in the shelter, seeming to plan to stay there. She did not want any further examination. She was in turmoil after what the storyteller and her grandmother had said. Both recognized her as having spirit connection. She barely understood, yet she realized somehow touching spirits bestowed power. Nobody in the clan or anywhere else ever treated her grandmother with anything but the greatest respect. Was it the spirit connection? Was it some power she had? Elka was uncertain.

She thought back to the wolf's behavior. Couldn't anyone else have figured out the wolf wanted them to follow? Why was that seen as spiritual communication? She tried to remember everything she could about the event. In her mind, she could see the wolf, lying there, whining. She could see it get up, looking behind. She could see it return to lie down at her father's feet to whine. Wouldn't anyone know, she thought, that the wolf wanted to be followed? Well, maybe not, she finally thought. It didn't seem to have occurred to the thoughts of her father or Sum.

She would have to talk to Matta. She needed to understand this spirit experience. She wanted to know first of all what was of the normal world and what was of this spirit world. She wanted to be able to separate in her mind which was which. She had honestly thought she reasoned the wolf's behavior, not learned it by some wolf to wolf spirit, to human spirit, to human communication. She felt a keen need to know how to live in two worlds.

Elka saw her mother, Dal, and walked over to her. "How's my girl?" Dal asked, not really wondering. "Upset," Elka replied. "Father hurt me."

"Oh, Elka," her mother said, "he has a complete right to do whatever to you or any of us as he chooses. He is the man. He is a good man. You must have done something else that provoked him. You've done much recently to provoke him. If he sees a challenge to his authority, he will not let it go undefeated. You know that. You should control your behavior better. I'm on my way to the creek to wash some things. Want to join me?"

"No, thanks, Mother. I'd have to have Father's permission to leave the flat top."

Elka wandered away, feeling aloneness for the second time in her life, this time in the presence of many people. Her mother blamed her for whatever her father did. Elka felt unprotected by both parents. Was there no one to see the wrong in her father? Even more, was there no one to do anything about it?

She sought Matta and saw the old woman in the distance near the forested edge of the flat top on which they lived. Matta was talking to Pagu, Sum's wife, and Reorg, Jin's wife. Matta was worried. She hadn't intended to tell Abu about Elka's spirit yet. He feared hers, and he would fear it in his daughter. That might make things worse for Elka.

Matta had stopped to share her concerns over potential problems with Abu with women strong in their support of each other. She wanted them to let her know, when anyone saw him treating Elka badly. Matta expected him to try to kill her spirit with power. Men would not like more spiritual power in the clan, he was sure. Already, he confined Elka to their hilltop.

Matta planned to talk to Bit, Lum's wife, and Wat, Elom's wife, before the day was out. She would not discuss anything with Koa. Poor Koa. She was outside the women's world because her husband, Hol, would demand to know everything anyone would say to her, and she would tell him. Women had few clearly defined rights, but they were very effective at mutual support, and that gave them a great strength. They would protect that strength with their lives.

Elka noticed Matta was about to leave the women, so she approached her grandmother. Matta recognized the child from the way she walked because from a distance all she saw was a blurry image. "Come with me," Matta said. "Keep your voice very quiet." Matta's lovely white hair was pulled back and tied with a short leather strip at her neck, unbraided. In the breeze little tendrils had escaped, and they danced in the wind.

They went to an edge of the mountaintop where pines grew thickly along the slope, rising above the flat top. The pines provided a buffer for some sound, while adding a delightful fragrance.

Matta asked, "Are there any people on the slope?"

Elka walked to the edge and looked down, "No, Tatta," she replied.

"Then sit with me," Matta whispered, "and alert me if anyone comes close enough to hear."

They sat on stones, Matta facing the view from their mountaintop, as if she could see it, and Elka sitting cross legged facing Matta. Elka brushed away the hair that had fallen forward over her face. She looked intently at Matta.

"I am concerned about Abu," Matta whispered. "He now knows you have spirit. That will make him fear you. He already is angered by you. No, my dear, not because you left home. It's entirely more complex. Your personal travel for such a distance required a fearlessness most of the men don't have. Your father could have assumed you didn't know the risks, but he taught you the risks. He knows you know them. The only other reason you would have gone alone, in his way of thinking, is that you felt you had no need of protection. You were fearless and could stand your ground. Notice that when your father went to find you, he didn't go alone. So, you are fearless and have spirit, and that unsettles his world. He's been taught that girls want to find a strong man to take care of them. Men think they must be stronger than you, to protect you. Apparently, you have a self-sufficiency that makes it appear you don't respect that teaching. It makes him feel less the man; you, more the man."

Elka laughed lightly. The idea was totally incongruent with any thought she'd ever had.

"Don't laugh; listen," Her grandmother admonished. "Your lack of respect for what he considers the core reason for his existence, to protect his family—that angers him. He has been taught he must have complete control over his little family. Suddenly you, a girl, has great strength and spirit power. He was unable to control your going to the carcass site. He thinks to control you now—severely control you. I suspect he will try to kill your spirit. You must resist despair. You must carry on with what is right. I am unsure what he will do."

"He already told me I must have his permission to leave the flat top. Permission has to come from his mouth, so if he's gone hunting, I'm stuck here." Elka sat there, leaning over, forearms on her thighs, as if resting from carrying a heavy weight.

"Is that all?"

"He told me, if I disobeyed, he would give me to be Barg's wife, even if I'm not woman. Tatta, I'd rather die. I would end up just like Koa. Walking dead." Elka was visibly shaken at the thought. Matta's hand rested on her shoulder.

"I understand. So, yes, he is already trying to control you so your spirit cannot have any power to compete with him. That is what I feared. Abu is a decent man, but he cannot be pushed very far without taking revenge in ways his brother, Hol, would do. Trust me. Don't fight with him. Remain meek right now. Build your spirit, but show meekness. There are answers, but we have to find them. The women here hold together like a fishnet. I have talked to Reorg and Pogu. If they see you harmed, they will let me know. I am with you, Elka. Be patient. Keep in mind that if things get bad, I am ready to help you leave with Acconomaku. He would guard you with his life. He is a good man, a man of spirit. If I ask, he will do it."

Elka put her thumb into her mouth and Matta pulled it out. "That's what I fear. Elka, you must be strong. Do not let these things cause you fear. The moon spirit and others have a plan for you. All will work, as it should. Fear not."

"I'll try, Tatta. I thought my father loved me."

"That's where it gets very complicated, Dear One. He does."

"What?"

"He loves you as his special girl. The special qualities that drew him to love you are the very ones that now repel him. You are growing to a woman. He wants you to remain his little girl, but you cannot. A fearless little girl is adorable; a fearless woman is a threat to life in our clan. A strong little girl is to be admired; a strong woman to be abased for opposing custom. He is confused about how he is supposed to feel, but because of our focus on integrity, beginning with a man's having good control over his family, he feels any challenge to his power is a threat to his control. A threat to his control is a threat to him. Do you understand?"

"I think I understand a little, Tatta."

"Good. Don't brood or look any different from how you were before you took your travel. That may be hard, but you must contain a greater strength now. You do not want to set off Abu. You could be hurt before I could stop it. Promise me."

"I'll do my best, Tatta."

"I will have you help me care for Acconomaku to heal his wound. You will learn the cures for different things. These are musts for your knowledge. You will learn to heal. Pay very close attention. Come."

Elka followed her grandmother to her shelter. She was slightly frightened over having to be so very careful around her father, but she had a little understanding and that helped. Until this time,

Elka had been guileless. She had just learned to be deceitful, pretending one thing, when another was true. To do this for her own safety against her father was abominable to her. She wondered how not to be frightened, when the one you are supposed to trust lacks trustworthiness. She feared on two issues, for to Elka, living a lie was deceit. It chipped away at her integrity. To speak truth to power could cause her to end up a wife to Barg before she was a woman.

She must not make her father appear out of control of his family, even though with Matta's plan, clearly, he was in the darkness in knowledge of his family. Matta was, however, filled with integrity, and Matta was leading her. Elka found that disconcerting. Matta, she knew, loved her and didn't want her to have a life like Koa. Elka agreed wholeheartedly. For that reason, Elka followed Matta. She would follow Matta, even if it felt on the edge of losing integrity, maybe even if she lost some integrity—as long as it protected her from a life with Barg.

Elog, her twin called to her.

"I'm helping Matta. I'll be with you later," she said, sounding much happier than she felt.

"Good!" Matta whispered, noting Elka's attention to the forced lightness in her voice.

Elka would begin complicated training in healing the moment she stepped into the shelter. Geol was in the shelter and he pulled Elka's arm so that she fell to his lap.

"Grandfather," she exclaimed, "I am getting a bit old for that, don't you think?"

"Little One, you'll never be too old. Give this old man a hug."

Elka did exactly what she was told, and, after what she considered sufficient time, she said, "I have to help Matta. I will learn to be a healer."

"That's wonderful," her grandfather said with a smile. "You're smart enough to do that. Pay good attention." He swatted at her leg.

Then began multiple visits to Acconomaku, lesson after lesson into the properties of plants and where to find them, dosage, especially for those plants having both beneficial and toxic effects. Along with the information, Matta emphasized repeatedly that the medicine must be used only for good, never to harm. She told Elka her spirit was strong, and spirits would retaliate severely, if she ever used her knowledge for evil purposes. In the back of her mind, Elka realized she knew how to poison herself or someone else.

As she learned about healing plants, Matta and Acconomaku also dropped comments that caused her to open herself to spiritual things.

After a moon had passed, Matta told Elka to ask Abu if she could accompany her on a medicine-gathering trip. He agreed, since Matta had need of help with such poor vision. He reflected that Elka had been much easier to control since they returned from the trip. His showing rough treatment of her body and the threat of Hol's son had done the job, Abu firmly believed. Hol had advised rough treatment, and it was effective. Abu believed Elka would do anything to avoid being Barg's wife. She was his daughter. She must obey him in whatever he demanded, and she'd learned.

Abu had no way to know that Elka would never be Barg's wife. Elka was busy helping her grandmother to replenish her supplies as well as to establish supplies of her own for her secret departure from the clan. Only Acconomaku, Matta, and Elka knew. Elka would not even tell Elog. Leaving him would be cruel to endure for her freedom, but to avoid Barg for the rest of her days was worth the pain. Neither Matta, Acconomaku, nor Elka saw anything deceitful in their plan. They did not look at their deception as lacking integrity, but rather they saw it as preserving Elka's life and spirit, as if somehow, spirit was of greater importance than obedience to a clan rule. Acconomaku questioned whether there was anything at all called pure integrity. That was a new thought for Elka. As far as she knew, she'd never broken any of her integrity until she left to visit the mastodon carcass. She continued to defend what she did, but that defense was reviewed in her mind only. It was dangerous to speak it. She was supposed to accept her break.

Ranu and Elka were at Acconomaku's shelter. Acconomaku had been strong enough to take the wolf for walks to strengthen her from so much inactivity. Teera had experienced having to rebuild muscles earlier in her life. She worked to please Acconomaku. She had been patient while he healed. Now the two would work to strengthen each other. They watched Acconomaku return to his shelter and lower himself to his sleeping space. Teera walked over to Elka and poked her in the side with her nose. It made Elka chuckle, and Ranu laughed at the sound of the chuckle.

Later that evening, Geol called all together. He said he would go to the mastodon site in three days. All who chose to go must be over the age of eight years. He added—even Elka who had already been there—was invited, in fact expected to go, he noted with a grin. Abu glared at his father, but he would not argue. Geol had authority over the whole clan. Mothers would remain and Hol and Abu would guard the women and children at home, Geol added. Matta's face showed no emotion whatsoever, but she realized that, if she had the power to plan the escape, she could have done no better than this.

Later that night Geol snuggled close to Matta and whispered in her ear. "I know she has to go. Did I do well?"

Matta squirmed around and hugged him with all her might. She took his head in both her hands and kissed him with all the strength she had. "It's killing me to see her go, but she has great things to do."

"I know," he murmured. "We raised two sons and gave them much love. They know how to take love but have no idea how to give or return it. They understand the rule of our custom but not the spirit behind our rules."

PART THREE

The day of the travel to the mammoth site arrived. Provisions were already packed. Excitement was in the air. They would bring back good material for tools, and they definitely needed replacements. Their discard pile, where they put things they no longer found useable, was filled with broken tools. For many tools they could have used stone, but they liked bone from mastodons or mammoths best. There was a sense of size, strength, and life to the bone. It's as if it exuded a spirit that stone just didn't. And they could shape it a lot easier than stone, except for Elom, who seemed to have a way with stone that none of them could understand, let alone master.

Elka had her backpack prepared along with blanket rolls. Elog was also well prepared. Acconomaku had his things from the wash, which accompanied him on the stretcher to the home of the clan. He hugged Matta. She shed a few tears onto his arm. She was happy, and her heart was breaking at the loss to come. No one noticed her emotional display. Each was too busy with their own packing. Teera sat patiently at the side of Acconomaku. She turned her eyes back and forth trying to take in what was happening. She remained patient.

Abu was in his shelter, enraged. He had not given Elka permission to leave, yet Geol had not only done so, he made it sound like an order by saying he expected her to go. Geol's power was so much greater than his own. He had no choice but to let her go. Elka stopped at her shelter to pick up the rabbit cape. Abu seized her arm. Elka froze in place terrified.

"You should have refused to go," Abu told her tensely, moving his arm to wrap it firmly behind her as if a hug to pull her to him, while lifting her tunic.

"Don't!" she shouted, infuriated, trying to pull away. Then, she paused, thinking she'd provoked him.

He was lifting her tunic higher with her back to the outside of the shelter, so no one could see what he was doing. She shivered, because he was lying with his body instead of his mouth. Those passing by would think he hugged her, never guessing what was really happening. She had no way to know what to expect, but she was terribly frightened. She thought he had a right, so she did not scream.

"Don't, don't!" she pleaded, quieter. Then, she said anguished, "That hurts. That hurts so bad." She let out a quiet sob. Tears began to form, and she tried to hold them back almost successfully.

"Maybe that'll teach you something," he said gruffly, not turning loose of her. There was blood on his finger. He licked it off, while staring into her eyes with a leer, a look that baffled Elka. Abu was shocked that he felt some enjoyment over her suffering at his hands. To this point he'd felt bad about treating her roughly, but this time, he could feel her strength give way in his hands. He liked it. It made him feel stronger, more the man. Her fear of him drove him on. Once more he repeated what he'd done, and she stifled her desire to scream. Again, he licked blood off his finger with a hideous look on his face, and she did not know how to interpret it other than hate. He released his hold. Elka fled the shelter, shaking, leaving the rabbit cape with what remained of her things in the shelter.

Matta found Elka, and gave her a hug.

"It kills me to leave you, Matta," Elka told her grandmother, "but I must. It gets worse."

"I know, Elka. Be strong."

"I will," Elka promised in a whisper.

She watched the girl go straight to Geol to stand so he could see her. Matta suspected something from Abu, but she felt Elka was now safe and on her way somehow to use the spirit gift she'd been given. Matta also realized that Geol would do his very best to protect Elka, as would Acconomaku—and Teera.

Geol shouted above the noise, "We leave!" He waved his stiff arm from his side to his head with his fingers pointing the direction. All participants began to depart. Elka left with tears about to spill out from her eyes. She bit her lip to cause different thoughts. She and Elog, her twin, did a few steps of their childhood skip-dance, and they began the serious trek. Ranu joined the two. They followed right behind Geol. At the very end of the trekkers, Acconomaku came with Teera.

The day was warm with a cloudless, blue sky. All were in high spirits, except for Elka. She tried to show a lightheartedness, but she wanted to crawl into a bundle to weep until her supply of tears went dry. Elka was certain that her father hated her. He wanted to hurt her. It broke her down, but at the same time it enraged her with a force that was formidable. She resolved to learn somehow to use her spear in ways that would make it possible to defend herself against him, even if it meant sinking her spear into him as into a deer. No one had a right to do this to another. No one. Father or not. She vowed he would not touch her again. She considered seriously that, if she ever returned, her father would give her to Barg. She knew she could not ever let that happen. She would not feel safe again until Acconomaku, Terra, and she were separated from the group, and they had traveled several days to their new destination. She put on her fake smile and walked just behind Geol, keeping time with the steps he took, and she began to hum quietly. She concentrated on the steps. Each step took her nearer to a new and, she believed, better life.

Elog watched his twin. She appeared to be feeling a lot better than she had when they left their home camp. He looked at Ranu, and Ranu nodded back with a smile.

Elka was surprised that Barg had chosen to remain at home, until it occurred to her that he likely didn't choose to remain there but had been ordered to remain there by his father. If for some reason the clan had to protect the women and children, two men would have a tough time of it. Barg could be counted on to help the men.

It took most of the daylight to reach the mastodon carcass, for they walked instead of ran. They had burdens of meat to carry along with their backpacks. At one point, Sum, Jin, and Sig broke off from the group to head to the rockslide where they knew they'd find some stones for anvils and hammers. The major part of the group reached the lone tree and turned off toward the mastodon site.

Elka thought momentarily of her attempt to make a softer sleeping place and add warmth by pulling reeds over herself. She would not make that mistake again. She smiled to herself.

When the group neared, all were stunned by the peculiar odor, carried in brief intervals on the light breeze. They turned back to an area where there was a slight depression bowled into the land and away from the unpleasant smell. That would, they decided, make a good place to camp. Geol had the younger men start a fire for the evening and night. Others carried much of the meat to the river to submerge it for freshness and safekeeping. There was some wood available for the fire in the forests that edged the area where the mastodon had gone down.

Shortly after they arrived, Sum, Jin, and Elom arrived laden down with stones for breaking the large mastodon bones. They took the rocks to the area where they'd break apart the bones. They had collected anvils and hammers. Sum and Jin went into the forest searching for a couple of sturdy, straight fallen trees they could use as long handles for the hammers.

Acconomaku went over to Elka, who was walking about unsure what to do.

"Elka," he said gently, "Bring your things over here next to mine."

She did, laying her spear near his. She shrugged off the backpack, and put it next to his. Acconomaku sat down near the backpacks, and Teera joined him.

"I think it a good idea for you to stay close to me for this time," Acconomaku said very quietly to her. He patted the ground indicating for her to sit. She complied. "It will appear that you are taking care of my wound, and others will not feel a need or develop habits to protect you, since you're with me and Terra. It will be easier for you to separate, if they are convinced they are not responsible, somehow, for you."

"I'll do it," she whispered. "I understand."

"As we left, you looked terrified. What happened?" he asked her.

Her emotions rose to the surface. Acconomaku knew all the things that happened to her. Matta had shared and so had Elka.

"You don't have to tell me, Elka. It's yours whether you talk or not."

"My f-f-father," she stuttered whispering, "my f-f-f-father made me stand still and he t-t-touched me; he pierced me. To people outside our shelter, it would have looked like he hugged me before we left, but he did not hug me. It hurt so bad," she stifled a sob and whispered as tears fell from her eyes, tears freed at last. She wiped them away, making a bit of a dirty mess of her face. "It made me bleed, and, then, he licked my blood off his finger while he looked hatefully into my eyes. He hates me. Then, he did it again. Acconomaku. I've never been hated. My own father hates me and wants to hurt me in cruel ways."

Acconomaku moved nearer to her. He wiped her face, so that others would not easily know she'd cried. "That's why you will leave and never return, Elka. Don't worry. We are going to make it so you're safe from him. You still have integrity, and you will have safety. The spirits surround you. Resist despair. Your father doesn't hate you, but he is a man with a sickness right now. That sickness is one he brought on himself. You are not responsible. The customs of your clan are responsible for the sickness. Where we go, it's different. People will not treat you that way in Mul."

Elka looked at him, shocked. Her father didn't hate her but instead was a sick man? He was well enough to go out hunting the whole day before they left. She thought the world was terribly complex. Someday, perhaps, Acconomaku would explain. At this moment, she couldn't grasp any of it. She kept seeing her father's face with that frightening, evil look in his eyes, as he licked her blood from his finger. She was certain his look meant he'd like to do it again and again. She continued to look to the horizon to see whether her father's shape appeared coming for her. She didn't see anything on the horizon. But she never knew when he might appear. She stayed wary and watchful.

Acconomaku understood her wariness. "Elka," he said at a low whisper, "I will also watch, and so will Teera. You are not alone. Trust us."

Elka permitted a small, very small smile to curve her lips upward. "I do trust you and Teera," she whispered.

"Acconomaku," Elka whispered after a moment. "Would he eat me?"

The question made no sense to Acconomaku. "Eat you?"

"His face seemed say he enjoyed the blood. I thought he might pin me to the ground and eat me a bit at a time until all my meat was gone and I was like the mastodon there, just awful meat and bones."

"Oh, ye spirits of the land!" he said louder and then silenced himself to a bare whisper. "No, Elka. That's not what it's about. It's about a part of life you know nothing about yet. I can't explain it right now. It's something corrupted in your father's mind now. What he really wants is the spiritual life in you to die. Not for you to die, just that spirit connection. It is something he doesn't have and cannot understand. He fears it. He wants you to grow to woman, and he wants you to remain child."

"Spirit is part of my life. If he killed that, I'd die."

"That's why Matta saw a way to save you, and we're doing it."

"I see. So, he's sick and feels healthy, and I'm healthy but feel sick."

"Yes, Elka, but as time passes, you'll know you're healthy and will feel healthy. This will pass, just as all life's terrors pass—eventually."

"I wish it would hurry."

"All in time, Elka, all in time. Let's go fill our water bags."

Elka quickly pulled out her water bag and raised herself to her feet. Acconomaku and Teera were on their feet and they headed off toward the water. Elka followed right behind.

"It was in plants such as these where you found the crayfish?" Acconomaku asked, pointing to the lotus flowers.

"Yes, I just moved the big leaves to the side and stared into the water."

"I don't know many people who would have thought to look for crayfish here. Usually, they're in with rocks."

"Well, they're here, too," she laughed.

Acconomaku gently moved some of the lotus leaves to the side and stared into the water's lowest level.

"See, right there," Elka pointed.

Acconomaku saw it, looked up at her, and he grinned a great grin. She'd never seen such a grin on his face. "Of course." He laughed.

They both filled their water bags and carried them back to the camp. Teera jogged behind them.

The men who came on the trek, Sum, Lum, Jin, and Elom along with Geol, had decided to bring a few complete deer legs so as to keep from having to stop work to hunt. Several complete legs had been submerged in the river water to protect them. Meanwhile, they roasted one of the legs over a fire to apportion among themselves that night. As the sun began to set, they gathered, and each received a portion cut from the leg by Elom. Each had a stick on which to spear the meat, if they wanted to cook it further.

Elka chose to spear hers and she dreamily held it over the fire. From time to time she checked the horizon toward home, and still there was no sight of Abu. He must have remained at home. Then, she realized that each time she thought she had figured him out, he'd done something so unexpected that she lost all trust in his having any pattern of behavior that she could anticipate. Elka kept up her vigil. Acconomaku would look at her from time to time and show her an understanding face without words. She appreciated that gesture, for it was comforting.

Elog and Ranu had spent some time since Acconomaku's arrival trying to determine what caused a change they could detect in the clan. They had crept up behind shelters and people who were unaware of their presence, listening to what they were saying. Elog had heard things that disturbed him greatly from his father's doing things roughly to Elka and talking to Hol about becoming a stronger man. The large amount of time Elka spent with Matta made sense, but it also made Elog consider that Matta would do everything to protect Elka. Ranu heard Matta say so to Acconomaku. Elog and Ranu had learned just enough to consider that this trip would be Acconomaku's chance to help Elka get away from the clan. Elog remembered Matta's words that Elka would one day leave and not return. The boys expected the traveler knew where she might be safe in a place different from theirs. The two had planned to escape when Elka did. They would go with her.

No one knew of the boys' plan. They had not figured out how to do what they planned and at the same time to avoid giving away what Elka and Acconomaku had in mind. Finally, Elog could stand it no longer, so he walked over to Acconomaku.

The man wondered what Elka's twin wanted.

"Will you walk with me to the river?" Elog asked him.

Acconomaku nodded and they turned their backs on the camp and began to walk. Elog had definitely roused Acconomaku's curiosity.

Elog was uncomfortable but needed clarification, so he started talking quietly and fast. "Ranu and I have been observing. It seems clear to us that you will help Elka get away to somewhere safe, for she is not safe from my father, who bears her no good will at this time."

Acconomaku revealed nothing of the shock that went through him on that revelation. Another of the twins just surprised the man beyond anything he could have imagined the boy wanted to share.

"We watched my father and Hol," Elog whispered.

Acconomaku looked behind them. Nobody was within hearing distance.

"My father did bad things to my sister—things no one should do to a child of his own body. I could not see it, but whatever he did hurt her badly, and she begged him not to do it, and he continued on. Ranu and I hid behind the shelter. It angered me, as if he did it to me as well as Elka, but I was powerless. I watched Matta and sometimes we spied on her and you. We know you plan to help her escape, and we are going with you, too. You know of a better place, a better way to live. Our clan is dying for lack of goodness. Ranu and I do not know how to escape with you. Please help us. We don't want to follow and give away your destination."

Acconomaku was appalled. He and Matta thought they'd been so very careful. He also thought of what Elka must have gone through. How he hurt for her. She was so young. Elog and Ranu had studied the situation and figured things out well. They were smart to know they had no idea how to join with him and Elka without giving away the plan.

Acconomaku looked into the sunset. It was lovely in deep reds and purple color with some yellow in the fading blue. He looked at Elog. "I will talk with you tomorrow." Elog left to share with Ranu.

Acconomaku sat for a moment on the sand, running his fingers through the tiny pieces of what he considered remains of former great hills, if not mountains. He had observed the disintegration process where rocks turned to smaller rocks and eventually turned to sand. Elka's face appeared in his thoughts. She was so strong in some ways, but, he knew, having been betrayed by the one whose job it was to protect her, she was also terribly fragile. She hid that part remarkably well. He was devoted to see that she did not crumble as mountains did to tiny bits of sand. She must remain whole. He would try to help protect her integrity.

He knew he had to be certain that he did nothing that would jeopardize her safety. He was horrified that the two boys had spied and probably were as aware as he, if not as wise, regarding what had taken place. He felt he had no choice but to include them. They remained, he noticed when he returned to camp, in the location where they had placed their backpacks near Sig, though Sig seemed to keep trying to avoid the younger boys. Elog and Ranu kept their distance from Elka and played silly games, laughing and wrestling. No one would suspect what they knew. They looked like young boys enjoying a camping trip to gather tool material—absolutely nothing more.

Acconomaku began to see that the integrity this clan focused on, though it had moral merit, it failed miserably in practice. Give it a crisis, and deception and duplicity were as common as they were in any other group of people. He knew of only one place where he felt Elka would be safe. It was a long distance to the north. It would be best if they could reach Mul. It was the one place where people were considered equal, regardless of who they were. It wasn't always perfect, but there was a caring among people for others that he perceived as genuine. They had undergone some terrible situations, and yet their mutual concern for each other seemed to grow stronger through the tough times. It was a happy place. He would strive to reach Mul with the youngsters. He had a moral obligation and a spiritual mandate.

Geol went to where Acconomaku was sitting. "Beautiful tonight," he muttered.

"It is, Geol."

"You needn't pretend with me. I figured out the plan, agree, and support you all the way. That's why I included Elka by name. As you can see not a single other girl chose to come with us. This is just not a girl trip. I knew Abu would try to stop Elka. I finally let Matta know I knew. How can I help?"

"It's become worse, Geol. Elog and Ranu spied and know what happened to Elka. They knew of our plan. I begin to wonder if everyone knows. They want to join with us."

"That does complicate things. You and Elka will follow the group home, but as soon as all of us cross the first hill, you will go wherever it is you're going. Don't tell me where you plan to go. Just do not cross the first hill." After we cross the second hill, the boys will tell me they left something, and I'll give them permission to retrieve it. That'll buy some time." Geol held his hairy chin. The white beard blended with the white hairs on his chest. They sparkled in the remaining rays of the sun. "I'll tell them the plan. That keeps you from drawing attention to you with them. Understand? You only have to tell them how to connect with you when they return to camp."

Acconomaku nodded that he understood what he needed to do.

"Tomorrow, I will send Elog and Ranu to the south. I will have them make it look as if something or someone attacked. Give me a few of Elka's things; some of yours. Maybe some pieces of backpack. They must get some blood from somewhere to make it look as if something serious took place there. I'll tell them exactly where to place things, so it looks real. Then, if we decide to search, I know exactly where to lead. Does that make sense? We leave here the day after tomorrow. Leave the details to me. You be ready day after tomorrow to leave at the tail end of our trekkers with Elka. Have Elka pretend not to feel well tomorrow. That is reason enough for you to be slow. Remember to turn away as soon as the last person crosses the first hill."

"Thank you, Spirits, for sending me Geol. Thank you, Geol," Acconomaku said with feeling. He reached out and slid his hand in strokes down Teera's back. She arched her back, glancing at Acconomaku's face. "Your plan should save Elka."

"Well, let's hope so, or Matta may kill me in my sleep."

"Old man," Acconomaku said with affection, "that's the last thing on earth Matta would do."

"I know," he replied, leaning back to look at the sky. "I don't know how I was so lucky as to have her for my wife. I couldn't live without her."

"I am sure she feels the same way about you. Someday, I hope to live in one place with someone like Matta. Until then, I'm a traveler. Geol, I have the answer for blood."

"For the blood? What shall we use?" The old man asked. His thick, white, stiff eyebrows normally immobile over his brow ridges, seemed to move up his head for a moment.

"Wait. I'll be back," Acconomaku said.

Acconomaku wanted to laugh out loud, but instead he went back to the sandy area, lifted the gut lid that kept rain off the contents of the backpack, and pulled out a roll of light-colored leather containing several pouches. One, the size to fit a curved hand, was filled with what appeared to be a darkish powder. He returned to Geol at the river.

"It's ground up, dried carmine bugs," Acconomaku explained. "Tell them to mix well with some water and stir in the pouch. It'll look enough like blood, so if searchers expect it's blood, that's what they'll see. Tell Elog to paint it on with stems. Not a lot of painting on the things. Don't use too much. Let some drop to the ground, so it accumulates in soil. That is good. Tell them to return the pouch to me, so they don't leave it at the place to give away that it's dye."

"I know what you're talking about. Those bugs live on prickly pear. They make dye that looks like blood. I've been fooled by it many times."

"Well, if you expect bloodstains, you could easily mistake it for blood. They need to get it dirty, so it's harder to be certain."

Geol smiled. He tied the pouch to the cording around his skirt, and went to his place to lay out his sleeping skins. He drank some water, more than normal, for he wanted to awaken early. The sky was covered with a brilliance of stars. Geol felt at rest about Elka's freedom. Each went to their place to prepare for sleep.

Elka's worry about Abu's pursuit of them to the site was turning out to be without merit. She had seen nothing of the man, and began to breathe a little easier. She gave one last look toward the horizon that led home, and seeing nothing, she closed her eyes.

Acconomaku noticed the constant vigil Elka kept and whispered, "He isn't going to come. He has responsibility at home. Remember when he came to find you, it was dark. He did not make that trip alone. There is only one other man at home. Hol would never agree to be the only man to guard the women. Neither Hol nor Abu is brave alone. Even if Abu did leave Hol alone with the women, Teera would warn us long before he neared this place. Sleep, Elka. You are protected."

She opened her eyes just a bit to see her protector's face near hers. A trace of a smile crossed her lips. She drifted to sleep.

Acconomaku looked through his backpack and pulled out some leather that was a close match to Elka's tunic. He tore off a piece. Her backpack was distinctive so he cut off some of it and took a piece of the wood that supported it. It had been specially carved for her. Inside her bag was a pair of boots for winter. He felt bad, but he knew taking one would assure the finders confidence it was Elka's, and it would lead the clan to the conclusion that she had met up with a bad fate.

Holding the things tightly, Acconomaku crossed the sand to Geol. He handed the old man the few items he'd been able to gather. Geol looked at them, smiled, and hid them under his bottom sleeping skin.

Soon the camp slept.

It was still dark, but the moon was full. Geol raised his head, gathered the items stored under his sleeping skin along with the pouch of carmine bug powder, and he walked to the place where Elog and Ranu slept. He didn't speak but rather touched the shoulder of each boy and motioned for them to follow him. They went to the water, where Geol finally felt free to whisper.

"Boys, I want you to go to the lone tree."

They both nodded that they knew the tree.

"Take this package with you." He handed the package of items to be stained to Ranu. "This little pouch contains the bodies of dried bugs. Yes, bugs. These bugs make a dye nearly the color of blood. When you reach the tree, get some plants with stiff stems. Put some water in this pouch and stir the mixture. It'll turn red. I want you to paint some on the things here so it looks like blood. Be sure no bug bodies stick to the leather or wood."

"That's Elka's boot," Elog whispered, as he reached out to take the pouch from Geol.

"Yes, of course. You are making it look as if Elka was either taken by force or killed by some predator."

The look on the boys' faces was one of dawning understanding. Having focused for so long on integrity, the idea of such deviousness was not part of their natural thinking. It was, however, received with delight.

"Don't put too much of the bug mixture on these things," Geol said quietly. If there's too much there, it'll look like dye instead of blood. Pour some into the ground in a few places. Use rocks to hold the things in place, so they don't blow off in the wind, but make it look natural."

The boys were grinning. They realized they were staging a hoax, though they didn't know the word hoax, and it filled them with a new pleasure unlike anything they'd ever experienced.

"Now, get your spears. Do you think you can make it to the tree and back here before the sun rises? Oh, I forgot. Take the stiff-stemmed stirring sticks and bury them at some real distance from the tree. You don't want to leave tracking evidence of what you've done."

The light of understanding passed over the faces of the boys. "Of course, Grandfather," Elog replied. "That should be easy."

"Don't forget to return the pouch to Acconomaku."

"We won't forget," Ranu said.

"Go quickly," Geol insisted, "We have tool-making material to gather this day."

"We go!" they both replied at the same time, leaving at a trot.

Geol headed back to camp, stretched out on his sleeping skins, and slept again.

When Geol awakened, the sun was just rising. He was startled that he'd slept. Usually, when he awakened, he remained awake for the rest of the day. Lum and

Elom had a fire going and had brought meat from the river where they had stored it, weighted below the water's surface by a log. The meat was roasting over the fire and the smell was wonderful. Geol had no idea he could be so hungry. He saw the boys peeking from under their sleeping skins, grinning, and he smiled. He noticed that the little pouch hung from the tip of wood on the top of Acconomaku's backpack. Geol stretched, convinced this would be a good day.

Acconomaku reached for some meat and kneeled on the sand next to Elka. "I took one of your boots," he told her.

Elka was surprised, and it showed on her face.

"With Geol's help we came up with a plan. Elog and Ranu have known what was happening with Abu. They will join us. Geol told Elog and Ranu to set up a scene to make it seem as if you'd either been taken or killed. I gave them some carmine to paint a bit on the items taken. The painting will appear to be blood. You'll find part of your backpack carving is also gone. Sorry."

Elka smiled slowly. She was surprised that Geol, Elog, and Ranu were involved. She trusted all of them. She was overwhelmed with relief that Elog and Ranu would join them on their escape. She had grieved losing them from her life. The idea of setting a scene to fool searchers appealed to her. She understood that could, hopefully, cause people to cease looking for her. She took in a deep breath and along with the scent of meat, there were wafts of pine from the forest. The astringent effect of the odor delighted her. The day promised to be lovely. She rose up to get some meat, truly hungry.

Standing next to her, Acconomaku whispered, "Geol said to act as if you don't feel well today. That'll make your slowness tomorrow understandable."

"How do I pretend to be sick?" she asked, wide eyed.

"Come to watch us harvest bone, don't participate, but sit with your sleeping skin pulled around you, as if you were a little cold. Occasionally, cough a little, not a big strong cough, just a little one. If anyone asks, tell them you don't feel good, even if it's Geol or Elog or Ranu. Someone might hear."

Elka nodded, reaching for her upper sleeping skin and pulling it around her shoulders.

Acconomaku walked over to the place where Sum had already attached a big cobble to a tree trunk which was about as long as he was tall, and he was fastening the other to another tree trunk. The trunks had a diameter about half the width of the man's hand from heel to longest fingertip. The roots were gone as if the tree had been blown over and torn from the earth. Limbs also were broken off. Both trunks would do well as handles for the hammerstones, he was certain.

All watched, fascinated. The boys had never been to harvest bones from remains this large. They fidgeted, trying out one place to view the activity and then another.

Finally, Sum arranged a large leg bone above an anvil. He placed the bone over the anvil so his hit would free the marrow. He wiggled the hammerstone by the tree trunk where it was attached. It held firmly. He stepped up, placed the tree trunk with the hammerstone in his hands, and he raised it carefully almost as high as his head. He came down on the bone and it broke but not as fully as he expected. It was a good strike, though.

Geol stepped up. "We're after tool-making bones, not marrow. The marrow is likely unfit to eat. Maybe dangerous. This carcass smells bad. It's warning us not to eat from it."

The younger men looked at Geol, as if the old man were crazy.

"I hardly smell it anymore, Father," Sum said.

"Sum," Geol said, through clenched teeth, "Walk to the end of the forest and return. Walk, don't run. By the time you get back, you'll smell it again. When you are around a smell for a while, the odor seems to disappear. It doesn't. You just get used to it. You should know that."

Sum was startled, ignoring the bone he hoped to raid for marrow, he laid the hammerstone down and moved the anvil to a different place. He put another strong part of the bone over the anvil and readied himself to break up that bone for pieces they could carry home—pieces that had nothing to do with marrow. He lifted the handle almost above his head and came down straight on the bone. It broke just as he hoped. Using the other hammerstone on the tree trunk, Lum struck another bone. It, too, broke as he hoped. Sum was miffed. Lum was just ready to accumulate the material for tools they needed.

Lum worked harder than Sum. The other men and Sig, Elog, and Ranu gathered the pieces and set them aside on the hill in neat piles, waiting to be pouched for transport home. As they worked, tension eased and finally vanished. Sum finally reasoned that if the beast were somehow poisoned, he didn't want to eat the remains of poison. He knew, like it or not, his father was smarter than he was.

Elka watched all from above. She watched the hammerstone follow the line made by the tree trunk. She saw the big bone shatter. And she felt a jolt within her. The bone made her consider the broken integrity she had within herself. Her lying and faking had shattered her integrity. She could no longer see herself as whole, entire, utterly healthy. Something in her had broken in her leaving the clan. Just like those bones, she thought, they could not be put together and remain whole. The mastodon would never walk on the bone again.

Then, a smile crept across her face. The mastodon was dead. She was not dead. Or, was she walking dead?

After much thought, Elka wondered whether every person didn't break some integrity somewhere along the way in life. Did all people, she wondered, have broken places inside, broken places that didn't show? Did everyone have broken places inside that still had their own pain to inflict on the person who carried the brokenness—years and years after some event occurred? Was it just part of life? Or did anyone walk through life, never having a reason to break their integrity? Could that be possible?

Elka seared the vision of the large broken bone into her mind. That is what my broken integrity looks like. I vow to remember it all my days. I want it to remind me that I must make my remaining integrity continue unbroken, for, unlike the mastodon, I live. I am sad that I broke my integrity. I want to hold the rest of my integrity unbroken. May the spirits help me! I have seen what I have done to myself. Truth is that, in the same situation again, I would do the same thing. I must leave. That's all there is to it. I love my father, but what he's become could turn me to a Koa, and that cannot be. Were I to remain, I would learn to hate my father and Barg. I might even break with the spirit of herbs and kill Barg or my father or both.

As the sun rose overhead, the men and boys took a break. They had a tasty treat made of ground pine nuts, flour from ground lotus rhizomes, bits of fruit, and honey. The sounds emanating from the first tastes were creating an almost musical effect around the carcass.

"Oh, you should have seen it, when we were here before." Sum laughed with the guys. He stood up and took a rib bone, holding it up as he would hold his spear. "I went over to the tusk where this piece of it dangled from the tusk you see in the air. I used my spear tip to touch it—just barely touched it, and it fell." The men were waiting for what caused Sum to laugh. "It fell pointed end first and it stuck in the ground. It stood there for a while, erect. Then it fell incredibly slowly to where you see it today. I am determined today, before we leave, to dig a hole for that tusk so it can stand straight up as long as it likes."

"You mean it just stood there on its own for a while?" Jin laughed.

Sum walked over to the spot right under the tusk that was raised in the air. He picked up the piece and showed it to the men and boys. Then, he shoved it down into the sand so it stood briefly. He put his hand on the top of it, to steady it, so it wouldn't fall. He removed his hand. "There, like that."

Jin put another of the treats from the basket into his mouth and groaned at the delight of the flavor. He stood and joined Sum. "I'll be happy to help you dig. He grabbed a freshly split off bone and began to dig around the bottom of the tusk tip. Sum moved the bone and began also to dig. Elom also came to help dig. Geol took another treat and savored it.

"May I have another, Grandfather?" Elog asked.

"Until they're gone." Geol laughed. Without a question, Ranu took another.

"Boys," Geol said to Elog and Ranu. "Let me show you something in the forest." They followed him, wondering what he would show them.

"It's not something to show. I wanted to tell you what to do tomorrow. You must get this right."

They put aside every other thought and listened.

"Tomorrow on our way home, as soon as you cross the second hill, come tell me you forgot to bring your tool materials. I'll give you permission to return to get them. That will be, I trust, the last time in my life I'll see either of you. I love you. Know that my love will always be with you. Know that your job is always to look after Elka. Someone, sometime may have her as a wife, but you are her clan. You see that she is well treated."

"Yes, Grandfather."

Ranu looked into Geol's eyes. "We will come to you as soon as we pass over the second hill. We will remember."

"Good boys," Geol said. "I'm proud of the two of you. Let me look into the forest for a moment." Geol assumed he could find something to show them in the forest that would make his ruse appear to have been a simple sharing.

On the rim of the small rise that led down to the mastodon carcass, Elka sat with her sleeping skin pulled around her. She noticed the men had begun to use the hammerstones with their hands now, instead of the ones attached to the tree trunks.

Sum walked over to Elka to ask if she was well.

"I just don't feel right, Uncle," she said as realistically as possible. She coughed a tiny cough. "I just feel cold. I'll be fine," she said lightly. It made her feel terrible to lie, but lie she would to avoid Abu and Barg for the rest of her life. She had made a choice that would affect her life for the rest of her time. She was happy with the choice.

"I hope so," Sum replied patting her shoulder. "If there's anything I can do, just ask. You probably should have stayed home," Sum offered, heading back to the carcass.

"Thank you," she said, and coughed, shuddering at the thought of missing this chance to escape, if she'd had to remain at home. She looked over her shoulder to the area where Abu, if he were arriving would be traveling. Nothing there. Teera came over and leaned against her. It made Elka feel good. She stroked Teera's back.

"Teera, you're a good wolf," Elka said.

Teera leaned a bit closer and then backed off, watching Acconomaku at the carcass site. Teera was not comfortable down there where men hit bones with rocks and walked all around in manners she found unpredictable.

By time for the evening meal all the harvesting they were going to do had been done. They would get an early sleep and be ready at dawn to return home. They would have a heavy load to carry. Some thought they might need to make two trips.

"I'm eager to make some new blades. Mine are getting duller and duller. They reduce in size every time I resharpen them," Lum complained, sweat still running from his hair as he cooled down from the work and ate.

"I want some points and a long blade," Jin said. "My wife wants some decent cutting tools for leather and food."

"Mine, too!" Sum laughed! "Sometimes I get to thinking about my tools that I forget hers. She taught me." He laughed.

"How's that? Lum asked.

"She made my dinner where everything that should have been cut, like the vegetables and meat, were all whole! She even served my meat too large for the eating stick. I asked her and she laughed, telling me that she had no more knives or cutting tools. I'd rather eat with my spear things cut up than to pick up hot food, holding with my fingers. She received her knives the next day. Believe me."

Geol laughed and the rest joined him. The children paid little attention. Elka thought it was good Hol wasn't there. She knew he'd tear into Sum for making the knives the next day. He'd call Sum a coward and his wife something equally as awful. She was so glad Geol had selected Hol and her father to remain at home to guard the women and children.

Acconomaku, having finished his deer, looked at the carcass and the tusk standing up in the soil beneath the sand. A good part of the tusk stood above ground. It made Sum laugh every time he saw it. The traveler walked by. It didn't strike Acconomaku as something to laugh about, but he considered he was carrying the weight of the safety of three children at the moment. Another time he thought, he might have laughed.

Acconomaku headed down to the river. He laid his skirt over low bushes at the water and stepped in, walking to the center where the water was deeper. He folded his legs and immersed his whole body. He took a hand filled with sand and placed it atop his head. He rubbed the sand against his scalp, covering the whole area, even behind his ears where no hair grew. He bathed with sand everywhere he could reach and rinsed the sand off with the moving stream of water. When he wanted to wash his back, he entered shallower water to push his back along the sand using his feet. He stood, every inch of his body feeling invigorated. He pulled his hair back with two hands and twisted it to wring water from it. Teera sat on the shore watching. When Acconomaku emerged, he picked up his skirt, put it on, and returned to his sleeping skins.

Elka was aware that her protector was bathing. She watched the horizon and still there was no sight of her father. The escape was so close. So very close. She hoped that all would go well.

Acconomaku returned, he touched her shoulder, smiled, and then went to his sleeping skins.

"The sky shows good omen for our trip," he whispered.

Elka looked into his face and smiled a timid smile. How she hoped he was right. She lay down and slept, feeling empty inside. Her life was changing dramatically.

Morning came too soon, Elka thought. It must have been the early sleep, she assumed. She raced off to the part of the forest she claimed for herself to make water and did so. Then, she hurried back to roll up her sleeping skins, readying herself to leave. Some were fully prepared standing ready with their burdens of tool-making supplies.

Geol walked over, saying a tad too loud, "Feeling better today?"

Elka shook her head to signify that she really didn't feel good. He put his arm about her, "Then,

119

Little One, just take your time. Acconomaku and his wolf will look out for you." Many in the line set to leave heard his words.

Acconomaku saw Ranu at the river, and he went to him. "When you reach camp, go to where most of the footprints enter the water and walk north in the water. Try to make no obvious footprints. I will owl hoot to you when I see you near us. Make haste." Acconomaku drank some water and returned to Elka.

"Let's go!" Geol shouted, and the line began to move. They had not eaten. They would not eat until mid-day. Clearly the load was heavy. They would struggle with it as far as possible. When it bogged them down too much, they would leave the excess in a pile. Then, they'd return for it later. They reached the area of the lone tree and cut short their turn toward home. Geol was purposely pretending to reduce the length of the walk, but, actually, he was avoiding the scene created by the boys to appear to be Elka's death or kidnap scene.

As the people crossed the first hill a few men looked back. Elka was walking slowly with Acconomaku and the wolf. Satisfied that all was well, they crossed the hill and ceased to occupy themselves with thoughts of the girl.

The line nearly finished crossing the first hill. Elka and Acconomaku were far behind the others. Sum looked back and noticed Elka and Acconomaku were walking slowly, but making progress. Sum crossed the hill.

Acconomaku looked at the young girl. "You ready?" he asked.

"Yes," she said, no regret or hesitation.

"Come on then, and walk as fast as you can where all the steps from today are, careful once we leave the camp to leave no footprints. We'll reach rocks fast, but we'll use the creek to hide our direction. Come."

The two turned quickly, heading back to the camp and then directly among the footprints to the river. They headed upstream. Meanwhile, the boys had asked Geol if they could return to get some of their special tool-making supplies they'd left. He granted their request with a wistful smile.

The boys ran back to the camp as fast as they possibly could. They knew the most trafficked area to the river, ran toward it, and stepped into the water, careful not to disturb the vegetation at the edge. They stayed near enough the fastest part of the water to destroy footprints, but not in the deep part, for that would impede their progress.

They could see a few prints left in the sand by Elka and Acconomaku. They smoothed the prints. Teera seemed to have left no prints they could see. Ranu noticed clouds gathering in the west. Usually such a sky meant rain, and that could be very good to cover up their trail. He hoped he was right.

Acconomaku also noted the clouds. He hoped for rain and guessed they had until sunset to reach the place he had in mind for the night. It was a tiny cave up on the side of a tall hill, almost a mountain, but not quite. It was a place where he could have a hearth fire and they could use some of the meat he pulled from the water where the men had stored it. After that they'd have to hunt. It was a great place to see whether they were followed.

Finally, Elog and Ranu heard the owl hoot. They looked and looked, seeing no one. Acconomaku stepped out of the forest. The boys jumped, having no idea they were so close and hadn't seen the man.

"Everything smooth?" Acconomaku asked.

"Very smooth. I did feel sad not to be able to hug Grandfather. I love him."

"I know you do, Elog. This has been a tough decision for you. Sorry you had to make such a choice."

"Well, it's done, and I'm fine. When we ran back, I saw the tree and the way we hooked Elka's boot to a limb is something they'll never miss. It won't blow off either. It looked so real with the painted bugs for blood. It would fool me!"

"Me too!" Ranu added.

Elka stood back in the forest with Teera. She knew all this was caused by her, and she felt terrible. She also felt joy that it was working as Grandfather and Acconomaku planned it.

"See that tall hill over there? The one on the left?"

The boys nodded.

"That's where we spend this night. We have to get there before the rain. Let's go!"

They followed Acconomaku through the forest. There was no animal trail to follow, yet he seemed to know exactly where to step even though they were in a thickly wooded area. Birds announced their passage.

Some animals they never saw skittered off. Though it was daylight, it was darker among the trees. They moved as quickly as possible, single file through the great trees.

Teera came to a stop, ears up, Acconomaku looked carefully to see what concerned her. Off to the right, where Teera focused was a giant sloth. That shouldn't, he thought, have concerned her. Straight ahead, he saw the culprit. It was a bear. He didn't really want to have an encounter with that animal. Acconomaku tested the wind. The bear would not know they were there. He looked down the long bank that led to the water below. They reached a place where salt water entered the area, and the land on which they trekked was high above it. There was, however, a little further ahead, a place to descend down that they could use as a pathway.

Acconomaku silenced the children. They followed him carefully. Teera finally saw the escape route and led again. They slipped down the incline with Acconomaku hoping desperately they'd see a place to climb back up later. They reached the beach and walked rapidly along the cliffside. An eagle sailed by overhead. It dipped into the water, lifted a large fish, and flew off. The eagle seemed to signal all members of the group, who suddenly became hungry.

Acconomaku ran quickly to the water's edge. He squatted and reached out to something. "Here," he shouted. Elka, Elog, and Ranu ran over. There was a long area of blue mussels all tightly growing. "We eat," Acconomaku announced. "Who has a boiling bag?"

The children had never eaten mussels or clams. They were fascinated. They went to see what they could use as a boiling bag. It seemed that they had many things between them, but no one seemed to have brought a boiling bag.

Elka looked up. "I can offer one of my sleeping skins," she said.

"That'll work, but we'll only need part of it. We need about this much." He showed her with his hands.

Elka opened her backpack and was surprised to find some additional things inside.

"Who put this here?" she asked, surprised.

"What is it?" Acconomaku asked her. He hadn't realized anyone had added to her backpack.

"It looks like one of Matta's boiling bags, and here's a bladder. I don't know what else is here."

"Let me have the boiling bag. Anyone here good at starting fires?" he asked.

Both Ranu and Elka said at the same time, "Elog."

"How about starting a fire here, Elog. We need some rocks for boiling. These blue mussels will make us a great meal."

"Come, Elka, we'll find some seaweed to go with it."

They put their backpacks down and began to hunt for the various things they needed to make their meal.

Elka walked at the water's edge. It was refreshing after walking on the rocks in the forest. Suddenly she saw a length of something green with a lighter colored ball on the end with roots. "Acconomaku, what's this?"

He ran to where she stood and said, "Oh, that's kelp. We can eat that. It's definitely edible, not my favorite, but it'll fill us up."

Elka carried the kelp while Acconomaku kept scanning the edge of the water. Finally, he hopped into the water and pulled up a large quantity of glowing green vegetation. "This is sea lettuce," he declared. "I love it!"

Elka reached over to pull off a tiny piece of the sea lettuce. "It is good," she agreed. "Should I keep carrying this?"

"Let me cut off a piece. You three should try it so you know how it tastes."

He pulled out his knife from its grass sheath at his side and cut off a mid-section of the long tube. He raced back to the waters edge and brought more sea lettuce. "This should be more than enough," he told her.

They returned to the area where Elog had built a fire and had the boiling bag filled with water. Little stones were placed near the fire.

"All of you come help with this," he said. They followed him to the mussel bed and he showed them how to separate mussels. They gathered plenty of mussels and returned to the boiling bag. They dropped the mussels into the bag and put in the rocks, using their tongs made of bent wood. The rocks boiled the water but cooled quickly so the boiling process was one of adding and removing rocks to keep the water boiling. Soon the meal was ready. The mussels had opened during boiling, so they were easy enough to get at, though hot to the fingers. Elka loved the

125

sea lettuce, but could not stand the kelp, thinking it was not the taste but the slimy feel to the food. The boys were delighted with all of it and ate and ate. They carried their waste to the water's edge to let it go. Elka poured the contents of the boiling bag onto the fire and took the bag to the water to wash it out. She rinsed the bag in the water and and tied it to her backpack, so it would dry more easily as they walked. Acconomaku and the boys heaped sand over the hearth area.

Acconomaku had seen a place where they could regain the higher ground, and he led them there. He laughed and pointed to Teera, who had returned up the path they descended and had found her food up there. She returned with a furry animal skin, but what animal, he was unsure in its present condition. Teera seemed completely satisfied and proud of herself, prancing about, tossing the skin into the air, and catching it before it hit the ground.

They headed to the depression in the higher ground that Acconomaku had seen around the bend. They found it, but it required a little more effort to ascend than they experienced going down to the lower level. Finally, they were successful and resumed their trek. The hills to which they headed didn't strike them as all that much closer. The children assumed they would still be walking in the dark.

Acconomaku knew this area well. He had recently been in this country visiting. The people of Mul would be surprised at his return. It would take many days to reach the place, though. He walked faster to see whether the children could keep the pace. They did well. The environment opened up into a rolling grassland. Acconomaku asked whether they could run with their backpacks. They all nodded, so he took off at a fast jog. The children kept up. It had been a while since Elka had run, as she'd been confined to the hilltop. She tired, but ignored it.

The tall hill was getting closer and closer. Elka stopped for a moment, and looked back. The sun was just beginning to go down, not touching the water yet. With her outstretched hand, she had four fingers between the horizon and the sun. She wondered whether they could make it to the cave by the time it was dark. Her spear was getting heavier and heavier and the backpack was painful on her shoulders. She turned about and continued at a run to catch up with the others. Her legs burned. Her lungs ached from the uphill climbing.

Acconomaku reached a fallen log and stood by it momentarily, and then sat on it.

The children also sat, holding their spears out from them, tip pointed upwards.

"See that dark area in front of us?" he said. "That's our destination for tonight. We will be there in a moment."

Elka breathed deeply, savoring the scents. The pine forest overwhelmingly reminding her of home. She was eager to reach the cave. Elka was very tired.

The four of them stood and began to walk to the cave. Shortly they arrived and Acconomaku checked to make sure they weren't sharing the cave with other living things. Elka laid out her sleeping skins and stretched out. She stared at the top of the cave to see a lot of black. She realized there had been many fires in this cave, and she found herself wondering who the fire-makers might have been. She sat up, remembering there was one more thing in her backpack. She wanted to know what it was. She pulled out the soft leather wrapping to discover eight of the treats they'd had at the camp. Elka was delighted.

"I have a surprise!" she said.

The others came to where she sat.

"Look at this!" She uncovered the eight treats. "Take one!" she offered.

Each of the others took one. They were definitely hungry. They moaned again over the wonderful taste. Elka ate one.

"Save the rest for a special time," Acconomaku told her. "And it's great to see a smile on that face. It's been absent a long time."

"That's right," Elog agreed.

"We have just enough meat for tonight. It's in this bag. Elog and Ranu, can you put together something for tonight's meal? I would like to climb to the top of this hill.

"Acconomaku, may I climb with you?"

"I thought you must be terribly tired, Elka," he said.

"I am, but I'd like to see the sunset from there."

"Sure, if you want to, I'd be happy to have the companionship."

Elka followed him, spear in hand, to the top of the hill. There was a large rock there, just the size for two people. Teera lay at Acconomaku's feet.

Elka sat there, gazing at an incredibly beautiful sunset. It filled her with an unspeakable sense of joy, a feeling she hadn't had since she could remember. It seemed to seep into every part of her being.

Acconomaku was also experiencing his love of beauty. The sunset was amazing. So was this child beside him equally amazing. She was glowing with a beauty he'd never seen in her. It was the beauty of a very young woman, not a child. Her spirit was afire as she absorbed the view, as if the spirit of the sunset came alive inside her, and the smile on her face conquered his every thought, sparking to his horror a monstrous sense of demanding lust. Mindlessly, he reached out and put his arm around her with his hand on her shoulder. Instead of withdrawing, she sidled up to him. There were danger signals going off in his thinking, but emotionally he was drawn to her as a moth to flames of a fire. He hugged her gently, kissed her forehead, and then removed his arms, extinguishing any chance of continuing to set off feelings for which neither of them was prepared. He shouted to himself where only he could hear, "She is a child! Control yourself!"

Elka stood and faced him. She recognized his reaction to her. She knew his feelings, as if he'd spoken each feeling in minute detail. Her spirit was wide open and receiving. She had feelings that mirrored his, though even she also knew they were premature.

"Acconomaku, I love you. I've never known anyone like you. I just want you to know, I love you." It was simple, honest, and disarming.

Acconomaku wanted to take her right there. He was mature enough to realize, however, that she was a child. What did she know of love? She was a child. "I love you, too," he told her. He leaned down, scooped her up, to hold her high, to hug her to him, lifting her way off the ground. "You're very special, Little One," he told her, as he returned her to her feet on the sitting stone, "and someday you'll make Ranu a wonderful wife," he said, harshly putting things in perspective. "We'd better go down now."

"It's not over yet, Acconomaku. Can't we stay until it's over?"

"No, Little One," he added to remind himself of perspective. "No. The boys may have our food ready by now." He took her hand, as if she were a child. They headed back to the cave. Acconomaku thanked the stars and every spirit out there that the boys were with them. Had they not been there, he wondered whether he would have restrained himself. He wanted to think he would have, but he couldn't be certain. At that moment he wanted what she would become more than anything else he could think of. Not as the child. He wanted her as the woman, on fire as he'd seen her. Definitely not a child. He purposed to make opportunities for encounters like this one fail to appear again.

Why, he wondered, did love of beauty such as they both truly shared run so rare in people? It was one of the things he sought in thinking of a wife. He wanted one who could share the things he held dear himself. This child was the only other person he knew, other than Matta, who understood that joy on seeing the beautiful. And it transformed Elka. How it transformed her! Then, he wondered whether it transformed him. That thought had never occurred to him. He shivered at the thought that she might know the truth of what just missed happening.

As Acconomaku thought about it, Elka probably saw him as her protector, and that caused her to love him. It was a different kind of love than he felt, he was certain. That complicated things. He would think of her love for him as child love, and his for her forbidden lust, though he admitted he did also love her as a child. He would list all the reasons the two of them made no sense. He would get it out of his thoughts that way. They were, when he thought about it, twelve years apart. Twelve years! He was more than twice her age!

When they returned, the boys did, in fact, have the meal ready and they had found armloads of chickweed in flower. They had found the small spring just beyond the cave, and they'd filled the boiling bag with meat they were cooking. They had also filled everyone's water bag. The aroma of the meat was inviting. They sat and the boys served them meat on their sticks. The chickweed and meat complemented each other. They all ate until they were filled and maybe a bit more. Elka and Acconomaku heaped praise on the boys for the wonderful meal. They slept to the music of rain.

The ensuing days were a blur as they moved from one shelter to another, all places Acconomaku stayed as he traveled. His mind kept creating the steps his group needed to take. They had been pushing each day to cover a lot of territory. It had taken an entire moon to reach this place near Mul. He was hoping to get to Mul that day, but they would have to travel hard, and he wondered whether the children were up to another hard day of trekking. They woke to a lovely day and took off early. As they traveled, they came upon a herd of camels. Acconomaku stopped and silenced the others. He crept up, spear thrust-ready, behind a camel, so close that it was unbelievable the camel didn't know he was there. Acconomaku speared the camel and it dropped dead at his feet.

"Thank you, camel," Acconomaku said immediately. Somehow, he realized, he didn't think to thank blue mussels for giving him food, but a camel? He'd never fail to thank a camel for its life-giving meat. They bled the camel, skinned it, and ate a leg roasted over a fairly good-sized fire after thanking the camel again all around. Acconomaku was fairly certain they'd never make it to Mul by dark, since they took time for the meal, but they were needing meat badly. This was their chance. They stopped to eat some hot camel leg, speared on their roasting sticks and turned slowly over the small hearth Elog made. The meat was so good, they groaned over it. They put out the fire, and determined to carry the remainder of the meat to Mul. They were back on the trail in short order, going faster than Acconomaku thought they'd be able to handle after the meal they just ate.

A good four fingers before sunset, they arrived at Mul. People came out of their shelters greeting Acconomaku with great joy. People were coming to hug Acconomaku. The children watched. They knew their clan would never have behaved in this way, no matter who the visitor might be. Elka watched as Teera left the group to wander through the place and visit a few people.

Acconomaku asked to see Mawanaba as soon as possible. She came to the entry of her shelter. "I thought we just ridded ourselves of you!" she joked. "Come in," she said with a welcome hug. She nodded at Lamo to relieve the gift-burden of meat.

Acconomaku was in her shelter for a brief time and then Mawanaba called the children to her shelter. They went, amazed at this warm welcome.

"I hear the three of you are looking for a place to live, a place where there is no threat to Elka. Is that right?"

All three of the children nodded affirmatively.

"Feel free to speak here. You'll find all the people here are free to say what they think, and they do."

"Yes, that's our hope," Elog said.

"Then, let me welcome you to Mul. You may stay with us as long as you wish. We will find a way for you to contribute to our clan, and you are free to make other contributions as you like, once you've done what we ask."

Mawanaba looked at a young girl who had red hair. "Tell Har to take these young men to the young men's place." The girl, Kap, ran outside to find Har.

Moments later, a boy a little older than Elog came into Mawanaba's shelter. He went straight to Elog and Ranu. "I'm Har," he said.

Elog replied fast, "I'm Elog, and this is my friend, Ranu."

"I'm glad you're joining us. Please follow me to the young men's place. That's where people our age and older live, until we find wives and build our own shelters."

They followed Har to another large building made of posts with what looked like grass atop the building for a roof. The grass was very thick and tied in huge bundles individually and then together.

"Now for you, Elka." Mawanaba paced around a little. "I thought to put you in the young women's place, but that's a small hut for girls who just became women. You have no parents' home here, so you will live in my shelter. I will be a second mother to you. There is an area behind that woven screen where you will have a place of your own. Put your things there. We are preparing for our evening meal."

Elka went into her place and shrugged off the backpack and laid her spear beside the place where she would sleep. She was startled to have acquired another mother. This one was amazingly different from her real mother. This one seemed to be the chief of the clan, like Geol. It had never crossed Elka's mind that a woman could be a chief.

When Elka came back into the room, Mawanaba and Acconomaku were gone. Kap told her to come with her, and they'd get something to eat.

"She mothers me, too," Kap said. "I think you'll like her. She's a great woman."

Mawanaba had led Acconomaku to a waterfall near her shelter. It made a lot of noise. She went there to talk over things she didn't want everyone to hear.

"How long are you here, this time," she said with a grin, dimples forming on her face.

"I'll leave tomorrow," he said. "I should share one other thing with you, my friend."

"Please," she said.

Acconomaku told her of the hilltop experience at sunset with Elka. He left nothing out. Mawanaba looked at him seriously.

"That has to hit you hard, my friend. Her joy in seeing beauty is what reached you? You want to share that part of you with a woman?"

"Yes. That and the spiritual part. She also knows spirits, as do I. You can see why I brought her to you. She's been hurt badly by her father. She's afraid to trust anyone. She needs to mature and find a husband, have a good life that she deserves."

"Acconomaku, what if that right person for her is you?"

"I am twelve years older than she!"

"What's your point?"

"Age matters."

"It matters now, my friend. Shortly, it will not matter at all. I want you back here at this time next year. Then we will see what we will see."

"You don't think?"

"I tell you I have no idea. I don't know spirits as you do or she does. I do know what love is, Acconomaku, and you wear it all over you. At least I can see it. You, my dear, hilarious friend, are blindly smacked in the gut with love. I never saw an example this obvious. This will, my friend, be fun to watch. Once, I thought we might be a pair. Our ages are fourteen years apart. Age at one point is no longer an issue. But love as you have just experienced is worth the world, if it comes about right. Don't cast it off yet. She will be a woman soon enough. You don't know what a year will bring. Do not leave here without telling her you are leaving, and that you will return at this time a year from now."

"I hoped to leave silently."

"Don't you dare, my friend. That's cowardly. Don't you dare. Swallow your cowardice, and let her know how you feel. How I'd love to hear that! I'm hungry as a bear. You?"

"Absolutely!" he agreed.

After they ate, Acconomaku sought out the three children. He told them he'd leave in the morning. He promised to return in a year.

Without showing her feelings at all, Elka was devastated. She had never been as keenly drawn to any other person. Acconomaku was indeed older, as he pointed out, but he cared about others, he saw beauty in ways that lifted him to fly in his spirit as eagles fly. He knew the spirits. The boys hugged him. Elka stood before him, her eyes downcast.

Hugging the boys, Acconomaku noticed Elka's long lashes, her hair which was loose and hung to below her waist, thoroughly combed. He reached out and pulled her toward them so all four hugged at the same time.

The boys said farewell, and they left for the young men's place. Elka turned to go.

"Elka, I'll miss you," Acconomaku said, wondering whether he should.

She looked at him with a face from which he could not gain any meaning.

"Is your word good?" she asked.

"You know the answer," he told her.

"You will return in a year?"

"That is a promise."

"It hurts more than you know to see you go."

"I know, Little One, but I must."

"I understand why you think you must. Does it not hurt you?"

Acconomaku looked at the ground. What, he wondered, did she mean?

"Do you not call me Little One to make yourself see me as a child?"

This one, he thought, was easy.

"I call you Little One, because you are a child!" he said with strong emphasis on the last word.

"I ceased being a child when my father treated me roughly and touched me in ways that were wrong. Speak only truth to me, Acconomaku. Have you never wanted me as you want a woman?" She paused. "On the mountaintop at sunset."

"I let myself get too wrapped up in the moment. My desire at that moment helped me see you as you might be, not as you are."

"You didn't answer my question."

"I wanted you, but I recognized you're a child. That's the end of that, Elka. I had a mistaken dream of you as I sat watching the most beautiful sunset I ever saw. It was just a dream, and I realized it, almost as soon as it happened."

"I will say again. I love you, Acconomaku. Not as a child loves a parent or brother. I love you as a woman loves a man. You cannot change love by calling me childish names. It is something I have for you whether you are here now or ten years from now. It's what I told you on the mountaintop. Let that enter into your thoughts as you are far distant from me. Let it keep you awake. It will be no different from then to now to a year from now. You don't have to return it. But from me it is there. I told you, because I wanted you to know. I don't know how to turn love off, and I have no desire to do that."

"And I will say again to you. You are a child, and I will treat you as a child, until you are a woman." Acconomaku moved his feet, as though wanting to run. He wondered whether she'd keep his thoughts awake at night, when it was time to sleep. What a thing to wish on someone else, he thought.

"I understand you through your spirit, Acconomaku. You and Matta taught me well. I'll leave you alone now. I know the truth. I've said all I want to say." Elka looked directly into his eyes all the way to the bottom of his soul. She was startled by a strangled sound, very quiet, coming from his throat.

"Elka, I trust you know the truth. I must follow the lead of the spirits and wait. I can do nothing else. I cannot be around you, until you are a woman, so I leave. That is how it must be. If I remained here I would want you every day, and know it was not time yet. That is agonizing. I have to safeguard what integrity I have that remains. Do you understand?"

She nodded, turned, and started toward her little place in this new land. She had no tears to cry, only a plea to the spirits to keep him safe and turn her to a woman.

He grabbed her arm. Again, as he had at the sunset, he lifted her off the ground, hugging so tight, she was becoming uncomfortable. He put her feet back on the ground, leaned down and kissed her, a kiss not on the forehead, but fully on her lips. Then he held her at arm's length. "May my kiss reach into your thoughts each day, until my return. May you remember this moment clearly, and be a woman when I return."

Elka was stunned. She put her fingers to her lips and looked at him slowly, making the picture she'd keep in her thoughts and memory along with what he said. She turned and without a sound went to her place in Mawanaba's home.

Mawanaba saw her. "Elka?" she called quietly.

Elka went to her. Mawanaba held out her hands. "I love him, too," she said looking right into Elka's eyes. "It's not returned to me, as it is in your case. In your case, it's a time problem. He will come to you only when you're woman. If he lives, he will come to you, for his thinking is consumed by you. He has found in you what he wanted for years, and it makes him crazy, because he must wait. Give it time."

A tear rolled down Elka's cheek and then another. "You are so kind to share with me. It really hurts that I'm just a child, and there's no cure."

Mawanaba chuckled. "Elka, the cure is time. Do what you must here. Live each day. Fill your heart with joyful certainty that he will come to you, but live each day. You do not throw away your life, because you must wait. Do your work, give to others who have a need, and celebrate whatever beauty you see. Uma is our healer. She will teach you what she knows. Your job is to learn."

"You are so kind. Especially to one who has . . .," Elka gulped. "Who has broken her integrity and run away from her clan. You are kind."

"We strive to be kind here, to think of the needs of others. We have a different way to look at life from your clan's integrity focus, where people can only turn worse and worse as integrity breaks and breaks and breaks. Your clan provides no remedy. When we can help others, it's our joy to do it, for that is how we grow ourselves to decent, not perfect, people."

Elka felt as if she'd been shattered by a hammerstone attached to a tree trunk as the large mastodon bone was, the bone they couldn't take marrow from. Her people, thinking to set themselves up for perfection, set themselves up instead for destruction. These people set themselves up to grow better—not perfect—better. What a difference!

"Off to sleep for you, Elka." Mawanaba said, hugging the surprised girl. "Don't be upset, if Acconomaku has already left when you awaken. It'll be too hard for him to experience another farewell. Awaken ready to start a new life here. Hope for an amazing future."

"Thank you, Mawanaba," Elka replied, turning and walking slowly to her place.

Epilogue

I know my face is full of deep lines and my fingers stick out at a slant now instead of straight from my hand. My hands make me think of sea turtles' front feet. My skin, once soft, is thin and shows my blood tunnels. I know I walk with a limp and have a forward lean and a hump on my back. My breasts and what's left of the meat on my body hangs down in folds, as if reaching eagerly for the ground—a bit prematurely, I'd say. Some hairs grow on my face, as if I were becoming a man. I don't see as well as I used to, and my hearing is poor. I know I miss some teeth and have difficulty reaching my feet, but I want you to know I have lived. Have no pity for me. I never wanted pity and don't now. My dears, know this. I have lived! It is with great joy I could shout, I lived!

When Acconomaku left me at Mul, I thought my world, which had begun to look up, crashed. Nothing could be further from the truth. Mawanaba, my second mother, gave me work. Learn to be a healer. Following Uma's instructions was my work. I learned well. My second mother also taught me how to be a strong, yet kind woman. You can do both at the same time. But Mawanaba gave me something even better—she taught me how to live.

Some people spend their entire lives trying to gain. They want things, praise, power over others, people to accept their ideas, to be considered good, and so many other things. What you hear from them is "I want." That is not living. It's seeing oneself through things or accomplishments. Things and accomplishments do not define people, nor do they live. At Mul people are concerned about others. It is not a self-filling approach but a self-giving approach they take to life. A child tries to reach a fruit on a tree. It's just out of reach. A self-filling person will pass by, possibly not seeing the child's frustration at all, maybe not even seeing the child. A self-giving person will see the child and call the child to them. Then, hand-in-hand they will go to the fruit and the self-giving person will give the child a lift up to reach the fruit. The two will part happily from each other and the adult and child will remember the event and both will have good memories of the other. That builds a place where people are kind to each other, not striving to best the other.

Mul's people have a view of life to find ways to improve themselves, not others, just themselves. They know they are imperfect from the beginning, that they will sometimes do things that are wrong, but when they do, they go to the person they wronged and talk about it, to find what they can do to make it better.

In my original clan, everyone started with integrity, and it wore away as mountains do, a rock and a pebble and a grain of sand at a time. There was no way to improve. The idea was to be born and remain perfect. That is impossible. My clan had no remedy whatsoever for failure. The remedy, when someone did something unthinkable, was to exile them. They had to move far from us and never return.

In Mul's world, people tried constantly to view choices as answering how their family and all the people of Mul would best be served by a solution. That made people really think hard before they began to speak of choices. They considered many choices. The winning choice was always the one that served the most people. Power rested in the hands of those who demanded that all be served well.

It was a new way for me to live, but I learned it and lived it. It does work when all the people struggle to make it work and keep it working.

Acconomaku returned after a year. I had to admit to him, face-to-face that still I was not a woman. Oh, I was beginning to grow some woman things, but I was not fully woman then. It was killing us to have to separate again, but we did. He went to a place several days walk from Mul. Elog said when things changed, he would let Acconomaku know. He'd follow the trail to Masusumala. Acconomaku took something of mine when he left Mul, but he didn't tell me. He took my little bird-like rock. See it here, made of turquoise and yellow gold mixed together. He asked a person at Masusumala to drill a hole in it. The man did a wonderful work of it. Acconomaku put it on a strip of leather to bring to me to wear around my neck. I've worn it every day since then.

When the moon spirit finally caused me to become woman, Elog ran the distance to Masusumala to let Acconomaku hear the news. By the time the flow ended, Acconomaku arrived to waiting arms. He brought me the blue and gold bird on the leather strip and put it over my head. We had the best life together. We had mountaintop, seashore, meadow, cave, desert, mountain flower, river, and so many other experiences, just the two of us. We savored sunrises and sunsets, thunderstorms, hail, even a tornado. But it was not always the two of us off unto ourselves. Those were our special moments.

We went from place to place across this land. Any time we heard of a child mistreated, if we were able, we brought the hurt child to Mul. Here we tried to let the hurt, broken, angry little ones find a new way to grow. It might take a long time but they could find freedom from fear in Mul, and many grasped courage. I know so many people of Mul, now happily living, freed from their past. We traveled widely and every once in a while, we found a child who needed our help. It was our joy, for the two of us could not have children. We rescued four tens of these children. Today they and their children are a huge number of happy, loving Mul people. Not perfect, just good, decent people. They have made my life full. I treasure each one of them. They cover this life-giving land for days and days of trekking.

Teera lived two tens of years. That is a long life for a wolf. We adored her and it was very painful to have to bury her sweet body. She is buried next to our home. No more wolf pups have been given us to raise.

Acconomaku and I were together when Mawanaba left for the spirit world. Oh, what a sad day that was. She had been in pain, and for a few days she felt better than she had in years. Then, in her sleep, she made a sound, and was gone. I lost my best friend. Her home has remained the place where the broken children come to start a new life. It is beautiful there and safe. The people who care for the children are special. I, personally, see to that.

Acconomaku lived eight tens of years. He was the best husband anyone could hope to have. I adored him, still do. I expect to meet him in the spirit life. He has been gone ten and two years. He died in his sleep. One morning, he just never woke up. I'd like to enter the spirit world that way.

Elog went to the spirit world on a boat in the ocean. There were several of them who were fishing off the shore. A big wave capsized the boat and it was just too far from shore for them to make it. Water was cold. None survived. People on the hillside could see the whole thing. It was strange to live without my twin. Only two bodies were returned from the sea. Elog's was not one of them. Sometimes I feel his presence, though he is not here. His body went to the sea and his spirit went through the spirit entrance to the next world. I cannot look upon the sea without feeling his presence.

Ranu, sweet Ranu. He met a woman here in Mul, Amah, and they loved each other dearly. They had six children. Then, one day Ranu was hunting and a large cat killed him. I don't know what cat it was. We could tell by the claw marks, it was a cat. The men brought him home. The cat mauled him severely but didn't eat him. Within a few moons' time, Amah died. Their children moved to the child home here. It was so sad. The children were surrounded by people who loved them and they all grew to be good members of Mul.

I am now the age Acconomaku was when he left this world for the next. His spirit was well prepared. Somehow, I think I will have many more years here, for what reason I don't know. I have a new helper to train. She comes here in a few days. She will be with the children, not go out on the paths to places all over this land. Some people like that; others don't. We will see how well she does with children.

And so, my life goes on. It is a good life. I am so glad I took that choice so very long ago to let my integrity break some, so I could escape what would have been a horrible life. Life here has given me a chance to try to rebuild some of that integrity I broke as the hammerstone fractured the mastodon bone. It's not a perfect mend of the bone, but I am strong and happy. Since I moved to Mul, I've never once felt a need to pretend one thing when another was true.

Life and the greatest spirit of all taught me this: we are all blessed. Even if all looks dark, those gifts are there. Maybe your gift is to learn. Then learn everything you can with joy in your heart. Soak up learning like parched land soaks up a good rain. One day you'll realize you are overflowing with blessings to provide others, skills to teach, gentleness to share, patience to provide those who come to ask of you. When we look at the gifts we've been given, not what we deserved, but gifts that have been given us freely, look to see if you have things that others need to make their lives better.

Do you know how to do something that another needs to know? Sharing the gifts we've been given is the biggest blessing of all. When we do what's right, all people have what they need—everything fits together. I've lived through some bad times, and, now, at the end of my life, I look back and see myself surrounded by blessings in extreme abundance. Thank you, Matta and Geol; thank you, Acconomaku; thank you, Elog and Ranu; thank you, Mawanaba; thank you, all the wonderful children who worked so hard to come out from the hurt you experienced and make Mul special; and thank you, sweet, sweet Teera.

To all I wish the very best. May you find boundless joy in life and see the beauty in simple things, when things are hard and when they are soft. May you fly on the winds of beauty, dance with wildflowers, see the glorious sunsets of the deep colors, and hear the music of the sky. May you live life to the fullest each and every day. May you say at the end of your days, "I have lived! I have truly lived!"

SPECIES NOTES

This section is for those who have a serious interest in science. Species in this book are listed below in the order in which they appear in the story. I inserted these names so that readers, who want to see the plants and animals present at the site at that time, can view the images here or Google them.

White-tailed deer, *Odocoileus virginianus.* For those who hunt or know San Diego wildlife, when the deer these people speared in 130,000 BC are mentioned in *Integrity, 130,000 BC,* I use *Odocoileus virginianus,* the white-tailed deer, instead of *Odocoileus hemionus,* the mule deer or the subspecies of mule deer in the San Diego area currently, southern mule deer, *Odocoileus hemionus fuliginatus.* The deer population of the southwest US was founded by the white-tailed deer. Mule deer are thought to have evolved at the end of the ice age, way too late in time for this story. See https://retrieverman.net/2012/01/23/a-species-younger-than-the-domestic-dog/

Image is in Public Domain

Dead-Eater Birds (Teratorn), *Teratornis merriami.* These teratorns were huge. They stood about the height of a yardstick and had a wingspan of eleven to twelve feet in width. They are thought to be a bit more predatory than California condors, because of the size of their beaks. They scavenged as well as sought live prey, such as rabbits, which these birds could have swallowed whole.

Image courtesy: Nobu Tamura CC BY 3.0

Mastodon, *Mammut americanum.* Mastodons were furry creatures resembling and distantly related to elephants. They were alive several million years ago and became extinct about 11,000 years ago. They ate rough food with teeth that had cone shaped protrusions to help them chew the tough fibers. Mastodons lived in North and Central America. They ate forest plants, including tree branches, thus making it easy to co-exist with mammoths, which ate from the grassy open areas using their flatter teeth.

Image courtesy, dantheman9758 CCSA3.0

Crayfish, Genus Pacifastacus, species unknown. There is great gap in history of crayfish in California. Two and a possible third species are claimed as natural to the Cerutti mastodon area. They are *Pacifastacus nigrescens,* the sooty crayfish, and *Pacifastacus fortis,* the Shasta crayfish. A possible third is *Pacifastacus leniusculus klamathensis,* the Klamath signal crayfish. Three signal crayfish exist—the other two signal crayfish are considered invasive. I will leave this science to further research and use literary license to assume some form of Pacifastacus was present in Southern California in 130,000 BC.

Image courtesy: Bo Jägenstedt, 2006, CCSA3.0

Sedges, *Schoenplectus californicus.* This is a rhizome-rooted water plant that is native to the area of the story. Stalks grow tall and straight and the flowers are scattered, not formed together like cattails. The plants grow tightly together.

Image courtesy: Forest & Kim Starr CC BY 3.0

Yellow Lotus, *Nelumbo lutea*. This water plant is native to California and is known as a food plant. It has flat, floating leaves resembling the water lilies.

Image courtesy: James Phelps CC2.0

157

Tree Frog, *Pseudacris hypochondriaca.*

Image in Public Domain

Field Chickweed, *Cerastium arvense.* Field chickweed is an edible plant and has astringent qualities for natural skin cell contraction.

Image courtesy: Stefan lefnaer CCSA4.0

Dire Wolf, *Canis dirus.* The dire wolf was a common Pleistocene predator. Compared to today's wolves, the dire wolf was larger, had a more massive skull but smaller brain, and light legs. It went extinct along with the other pre-ice age animals.

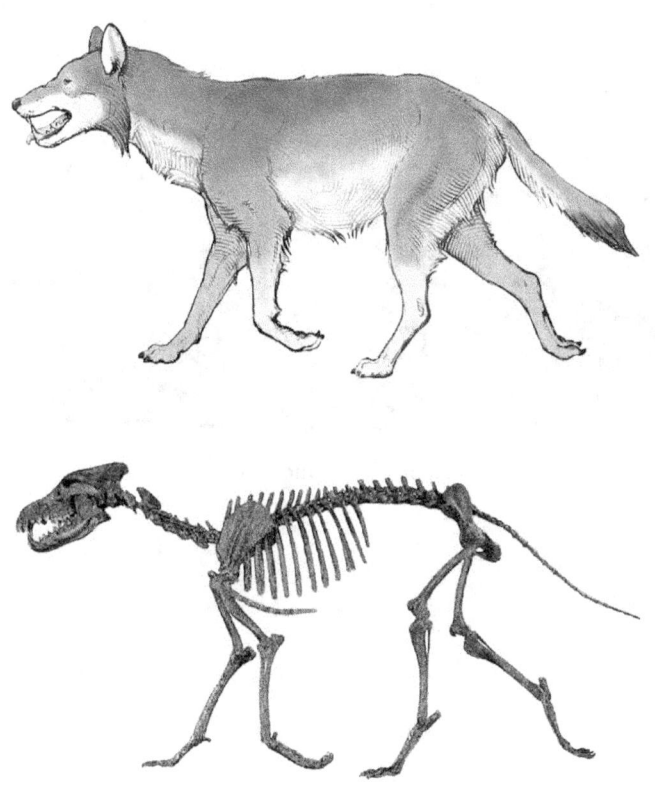

Image in Public Domain

Mesquite, *Prosopis juliflora.* This plant is indigenous to the area of this story. It has multiple uses by natives including: foods, eye wash, antiseptic, relief of chapped skin, headaches, making glue, and hair dye.

Image is in Public Domain

Desert Sage, Salvia. There are a wide number of different species of salvia in the area of this story. The one illustrated here is *Salvia clevelandii*. Desert sage has a number of native medicinal uses including: pain relief, antiseptic, poultice, sedative, and others.

Image courtesy Stan Shebs CCSA3.0

Plantain, *Plantago erecta* This plantain is tiny and may have been used by natives for a variety of reasons as plantains seem to share some uses. Interestingly, a few years ago, these plantain seeds were grown commercially as an important grain product for eating.

Image in Public Domain

Yarrow, *Achillea millefolium.* Among other uses yarrow has been used as an antiseptic, vasodilator, antispasmodic, and stimulant.

Image courtesy H. Zell CCSA3.0

Globe Mallow, *Sphaeralcea ambigua.* A native to the area where the story takes place, this plant is used as a tea from the leaves for sore throats. It's important to strain it thoroughly through something to catch the hairs that cover the leaves, because they can irritate the throat you're trying to soothe. It is also used for infections, wounds, snakebites, and as a poultice.

Image courtesy Stan Shebs CCSA3.0

Prickly Pear Cactus, *Opuntia littoralis.* This plant has many uses, but today the main uses are for treating diabetes, reducing cholesterol, In the past it was used as an anti-inflammatory.

Image is in Public Domain

Steppe Bison, *Bison priscus.* This bison came across Beringia and traveled the western part of North America to Mexico during the Pleistocene. It was a source of meat for those who could successfully spear one or find a corpse to scavenge.

Image courtesy Robert Pawlicki CCSA4.0

Short-Faced Bear, Arctodus. The short-faced bear is one of the top predators during the Pleistocene. They were the largest bear and are thought to have been the fastest runner of the bears, making speeds of 40 miles per hour. On all fours, they could look a six-foot-tall man in the eye. Standing on its hind legs it could have measured twelve feet high. By raising its arms up, it could have reached fourteen feet above the ground. That's a huge bear!

Image courtesy Billy Hathorn CC BY 3.0

American lion, *Pantera leo atrox.* There is some discussion among scientists as to whether the American lion is a tiger or a lion. For the purpose of this book, the view is American lion, subject to change if and when the scientific community comes to a consensus. It was a significant Pleistocene predator with a three-to-four-million-year fossil record. This species is also called the American equivalent of the cave lion.

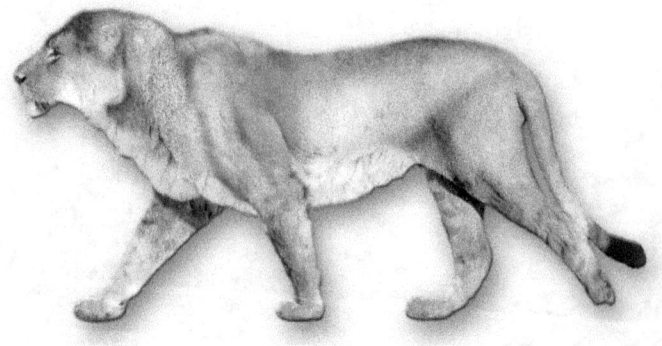

Image courtesy dantheman9758 CCSA3.0

Saber-Toothed Cat, Smilodon. The saber-toothed cat goes back a couple of million years. It is thought to have been an ambush predator, inhabiting forests and their edges and extending to brushy plains.

Sergiodlarosa, CCSA3.0

Carmine Bugs, *Dactylopius cochineal.* Carmine bugs live on prickly pear cactus in desert environments. They are filled with carmine, a red substance that is used today in dye for cloth and a coloring for food. If you see carmine listed as a food ingredient, this bug is the source. It enhances the color of strawberries and cherries. For a real red color either this natural source or a synthetic colorant is used. Had they been so inclined, ancients could have used the bugs to stain their skin, clothing, tools, or anything they chose.

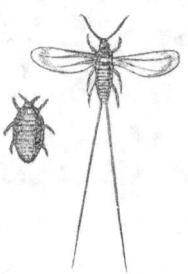

Image in Public Domain

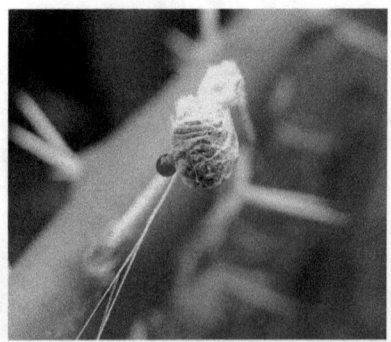

Image courtesy gailhampshire CCSA2.0

Bald Eagle, *Haliaeetus leucocephalus.* The bald eagle is a predatory bird that ranges from Alaska and Canada to the United States to Mexico. It prefers to live near large bodies of open water where there are old-growth trees for nesting. Their nests tend to be huge and weighty, requiring strong support.

Image is in Public Domain

Blue Mussels, *Mytilus trossulus.* Blue mussels are a salt water bivalve (two sides to the shell) and live packed together, as if they prefer tight social groupings, shoulder to shoulder tight. They have a byssal thread which looks like a thin string with which they anchor themselves to the area where they live or each other. The blue mussels that live on the Pacific coast of the USA look like the blue mussels in the UK, but they are entirely different species.

Image courtesy brewbooks CCSA2.0

Kelp, *Macrocystis pyrifera.* Kelp is an amazing marine plant that grows in long wide strands with an anchor at the bottom. It is a member of the brown seaweed family. Kelp can grow up to 150 feet long and in ideal conditions can grow two feet in length a day. Kelp grows in forests of strands. It is an edible plant and a great source of iodine. Some people harvest it and eat it. The slimy feel of the plant drives some eaters away, despite its being a great source of iodine, an essential nutrient it supplies generously.

Image is in Public Domain

Camel, Camelops. This camel is thought to have arisen in North America, going extinct at the end of the last ice age glaciation event.

Image courtesy sergiodlarosa CC BY 3.0

Giant Sloth, Megatherium. This twenty-foot-tall adult vegetarian grazed trees. It was able to defend itself with enormous claws.

Image is in Public Domain

BIBLIOGRAPHY

Allmon, WD, Nester, PL, Mastodon paleobiology, tapho-
nomy, and paleoenvironment in the late Pleistocene of
New York State: studies of the Hyde Park, Chemung,
and North Java Sites. *Palaeontographica Americana,*
No. 61 (2008)

Fisher, D, Mastodon butchery by North American Paleo-
Indians. *Nature,* Vol. 308, 271—272 (1984)

Gaudzinski, S, *et al.* The use of Proboscidean remains in
every-day Paleolithic life. *Quat Int* Vol. 126-128, 179—
194 (2005)

Hoffecker, J, *et al.* Evidence for kill-butchery events of early
Upper Paleolithic age at Kostenki, Russia. *J Arch Sci* 37,
1073—1089 (2010)

Holden, S, *et al.* A 130,000-year-old archaeological site in
southern California, USA. *Nature* Vol. 544, 479—483
(2017)

Pickering, T, *et al.* Experimental patterns of hammerstone
percussion damage on bones: implications for inferences
of carcass processing by humans. *J Arch Sci* 33, 459--469
(2006)

https://arstechnica.com/science/2018/02/debate-heats-
 up-over-whether-130000-year-old-bones-were-broken-
 by-humans/

https://www.sdnhm.org/blog/blog_details/the-cerutti-
 mastodon-site-one-year-later/96/

http://www.latimes.com/local/california/la-me-cerutti-
 mastodon-20171222-htmlstory.html

https://iafi.org/the-cerutti-mastodon-site-a-bretz-type-
 controversy-of-our-time/

https://news.nationalgeographic.com/2017/04/mastodons-
 americas-peopling-migrations-archaeology-science/

https://www.sandiegoreader.com/events/2017/nov/28/the-
 cerutti-mastodon-site-evidence-/#

http://www.sci-news.com/archaeology/cerutti-mastodon-
 site-humans-north-america-04815.html

https://news.umich.edu/mastodon-discovery-in-san-
 diego-shakes-up-our-understanding-of-early-humans-
 in-the-new-world/

https://news.umich.edu/mastodon-discovery-in-san-
 diego-shakes-up-our-understanding-of-early-humans-
 in-the-new-world/

https://www.nature.com/articles/d41586-018-01713-y

https://www.newscientist.com/article/2129042-first-
 americans-may-have-been-neanderthals-130000-
 years-ago/

https://www.youtube.com/watch?v=xvpwlnzzniY

https://retrieverman.net/2012/01/23/a-species-younger-
 than-the-domestic-dog/